MW00945175

The Rose & The Ring

Book 3

Lady Veronika

Joyce Brandt Williams

DEDICATION

To my husband, Paul, who challenged me to write, believing I could do it, and to my parents, Ron and Esther Brandt, who first showed me God's love and who tell everyone they meet about my books!

RECOGNITION:

To Devorah Nelson, www.storydoctor.blogspot.com, for her help with character development, story structure and editing; and to Aimee Stewart, www.foxfires.com, for creating the cover art for The Rose & The Ring series using public domain paintings by John Waterhouse. I am indeed grateful!

Cover art: *Fair Rosamund* by John Waterhouse

AUTHOR'S NOTE

In all our travels through more than twenty countries of the world, my favorite city is Prague, Czech Republic. Because it's the only European capitol never destroyed by war, Prague's rich history is still a living thing. The womb of a reformation that took place a hundred years before Martin Luther set into motion the Protestant movement, Prague served as a stepping-stone in moving the Christian church out of the Dark Ages of superstition, illiteracy and fear.

Jan Hus, curate for Bethlehem Chapel and rector at Charles University first university in central /eastern Europe, offering instruction in both German and Czech), taught the Scriptures to the students and parishioners. In turn, they permeated their culture.

Jan Hus introduced serving both elements of communion, the bread *and* the cup, to the common people and offering Mass in their native language. Home prayer groups, known as United Fellowships, were initiated by Jan Hus and emphasized missionary outreach and beautiful worship music. *Fairest Lord Jesus*, a hymn still sung today—and my all-time favorite—was written by a follower of Jan Hus.

Eventually burned at the stake by fanatical political/religious leaders, Jan Hus serves as a historic witness that true believers forgive, no matter how dear the cost. I could think of no better setting for a story about forgiveness than Prague, the city of Jan Hus.

On another note, to promote the flavor of the culture, I sprinkled in a few Czech words, and here are their definitions:

Koláče: yeast buns filled with a sweet or savory
Slunicko: sunshine
Teta: auntie
Dívčí: dearie
Bella Venezia: (Ital.) variation of Snow White fairytale
Tabard: man's short sleeveless coat worn over a shirt
Pani: Mrs.
můj bože: my goodness!
Pattens: wood platforms tied to shoes to keep feet dry
Cotte: outer dress/gown
Vanocka: braided raisin bread
vosi hnizda: nutty chocolate, cream-filled "wasp nest"
objets d'art: (French) works of art

—Joyce Brandt Williams

*Love is
friendship set on fire.*
—Jeremy Taylor

CHAPTER ONE

October 1456
Prague, Czechia, Kingdom of Bohemia

"Three *koláče*, please." Veronika inhaled the yeasty smell of freshly baked bread and flashed a warm smile at her friend, Hana Sikora, the shopkeeper in the little corner bakery on Celetna Street. She fished in her brown drawstring bag for the several Czech hellers to pay for her purchase while Hana retrieved the tray of freshly-baked, jam-filled buns.

Veronika placed the appropriate coins on the counter. "How is your father, Hana?" Even after a long day on her feet as a housemaid at a boarding house in New Town, Prague's growing residential sector, Veronika's inquiry lilted with good cheer.

"His cough seems a little better today," Hana answered optimistically. "Thank you for asking."

When Dasha, Hana's pixie-faced three-year-old daughter, peeked around the doorway leading to the family living quarters above the shop, Veronika quickly teased, "I spy!" as her dancing brown eyes played peek-a-boo between her yarn-swathed fingers. Dasha giggled and bobbed out of sight.

The sleigh bells hanging on the door jingled, announcing more customers. A girl of about ten years old bounded eagerly into the shop as Veronika turned toward the door. The child's scarlet cloak with a white rabbit collar and matching fur hat framed her rosy cheeks and emphasized her cherubic face. Her vivid green eyes darted straight to the pastry display—and her feet, encased in rabbit fur-trimmed black boots, followed.

Wrapped in sable mink, a tall, slender woman swept over the threshold and followed the girl inside. A light sprinkling of tawny freckles accented the woman's shapely nose, and a smile curved her russet lips. Her green eyes sparkled as she watched her daughter. But it was her gleaming coppery-red hair escaping from the edges of her sable hat that made her unforgettable.

"Choose four, Lucina. We'll save them until after our evening meal." Affection laced the woman's low, mellow tone.

Suddenly aware that she was staring, Veronika quickly turned back to the counter in time to see a toddler-size flash of blue dart from the family doorway to the end of the counter.

"How are you, *Slunicko*?" Veronika affectionately called Hana's little daughter "sunshine." "Have you been helping your mama this morning?"

Dasha giggled, offering a baby-toothed smile as she edged her way around the end of the counter. "I see you tonight, *Teta* Roni?" she asked in a loud, childish whisper, skip-hopping on first one foot and then the other.

"Oh, yes. I wouldn't miss Fellowship for anything." Veronika bent down and reached out to embrace the precocious child who had called her "auntie."

When Dasha flew to her, wrapping her chubby arms around Veronika's legs in a tight hug, she scooped up the child and nuzzled her neck with kisses while Dasha squealed in delight. Giving the little girl one last kiss on her up-turned nose, Veronika landed her on her feet and patted the top of her curly head.

As the child dashed behind the counter, Veronika picked up her parcel. "See you tonight, Hana," she said and then winked at Dasha, who was peeking mischievously around the counter at her.

Casting one last glance at the striking woman and her adorable daughter, Veronika opened the door and stepped out onto Celetna Street. With a gasp at the bitterly cold air that made her eyes water, she hurried toward the Stone Bridge.

Winter would not be long in coming; the bitter cold was intensified by a vicious arctic wind that whipped loose strands of Veronika's golden hair across her face. But she hardly noticed for thinking about the beautiful woman. How could anyone be so lovely? Why, even her voice was music . . . like soft notes bowed on a violin. She must be someone special. A nobleman's wife. Or even a princess. Maybe she lived in the castle up on the hill.

As she pulled her shabby cloak closer to her slender body, Veronika chuckled at her fanciful imagination. Then picking up her pace, she scurried over the Stone Bridge and climbed the hill toward her home in Lesser Town, the city's poorest section grown up next to Prague Castle's wall for the security it offered the unskilled and impoverished.

Veronika pushed open the door to the two-room timber dwelling where she lived with Antonin and Jana Karska, the couple who'd taken her in when her

12

mother died in childbirth. They'd cared for her with all the love stored in their hearts after they'd lost their only child in infancy.

"Shh. Jana is napping," Antonin whispered, shuffling to meet her. "Here. Let me help you with your things." He waggled his scraggly white brows and dropped his gaze to the lumps in the market bag that Jana had made for her in loosely woven stitches. Knowing her dislike of pickled herring, he teased, "Been to the fish market?"

"Why, yes." Veronika flashed him a conspiratorial smile over their longstanding joke. "I couldn't resist the briny smell." They stifled their shared laughter.

Coming from the silver-haired little woman supposedly sleeping in her chair, "So, the pickled herring called your name again, did it?" she chirped.

The three of them burst into chuckles as Jana rose to her feet. "I always say happiness makes people healthy. Must be why we're nimble as chooks, even at our age, don't you think, Antonin?" As Veronika produced the *koláče,* the old woman's bright, beady eyes twinkled in her age-wrinkled face.

13

Veronika bestowed a warm smile on the only mother she'd ever known. Nimble as chickens! Never mind that Jana was forgetful and Antonin was a bit near-sighted and shuffled when he walked.

The two women bustled between the work bench and the fireplace as they prepared the evening meal. Steam from the kettle suspended on a hook over the fire filled the room with the comforting aroma of mint and thyme. Vegetable pottage, one of Veronika's favorites, had been prepared by Jana. The aroma alone made her stomach growl, which caused Jana to chuckle fondly as she tumbled raw cheese curds into a roughly-hewn wooden bowl.

While he waited for the women to announce that the meal was ready, Antonin, who was sitting near the table, got to his feet. Reaching out, he picked up the hammered tin cup that held a single yellow rose.

Sylvia, the flower lady who sat daily from May to mid-October in front of Old Town Hall, had pressed her last flower into Veronika's mittened hands when she passed by on her way home yesterday evening, and said with a smile, "It's pretty—like you, *Dívčí*."

Antonin made his way across the room, lifted the dipper from the water pail, and carefully ladled water into the mouth of the makeshift vase. As Veronika watched him, she remembered humming under her breath as she walked toward home carrying the rose, her head bent to breathe in its sweet scent. Her heart had throbbed with thanksgiving to God; He alone knew how much she loved beautiful things—and how few she had. Nothing of any value, really, except the little ring that had belonged to her mother, which she wore only to Thursday night Fellowship meetings and Sunday morning services.

Antonin plunged the dipper back into the water pail and shuffled back to the table. He placed the tin cup holding the rose in the middle of the table and slowly lowered himself into his chair, listening with doting pleasure to Veronika's lively chatter as she retrieved the sweet rolls from the market bag and placed them on a brown earthenware charger.

"Today I saw the most beautiful lady ever," she informed them. "She has coppery-red hair. And her eyes are as green as emeralds—well, as green as I imagine emeralds to be," she amended with a laugh. "She was wearing a sable cloak and matching hat, and she had an adorable little girl with her; I assumed she was her daughter. She called her Lucina." Veronika's gaze wandered off into space. "And her voice . . ."

15

Looking up to find Antonin's eyes on her, Veronika cheeks grew rosy under his doting gaze, and she admitted rather sheepishly, "I imagined she might be a nobleman's wife . . . or maybe even a princess."

"You go on with admiring her, Roni, but *we* think *you're* the most beautiful girl in the world. When your hair shines all golden in the sun and your big brown eyes look at us, so filled with loving . . ." Antonin's voice choked, and he reached up an arthritis-twisted index finger to brush away a tear.

Veronika rushed over to the gentle old man and dropped to her knees beside him. Throwing her slender arms around his sloping shoulders in a big hug, she exclaimed, "Oh, Antonin, you dear. I'm so glad God put me in your home. Nobody could love me more than you and Jana."

"Come now, you two. This pottage is about to be cold." Jan quickly brought them back to earth. Her affection ran every bit as deeply as her husband's, but she was the practical one.

"We're coming." Veronika stood and scooted Antonin's chair up to the table.

When the three of them were seated, Antonin

said a prayer, speaking to God like a close friend. "Our dear Father in heaven, we, Your children, are most grateful for this meal. Bless it and us to Thy service. In the name of the Father and the Son and the Holy Spirit. Amen."

A little while later, as they finished eating Jana observed, "It will take some hurry not to keep the Marenkova's waiting." She began clearing the table. "I'll tidy up here so you can be ready to go when they come for you."

With a grateful nod, Veronika slipped behind the wool curtain that closed off her sleeping space from the main room. She poured a stream of chamomile infused water into the battered basin that rested on the stool beside her bed and quickly rinsed her face and hands. Refreshed, she dried them with a much-mended cloth retrieved from a peg protruding from the wall above the basin.

Picking up her stiff bristle brush, she wielded it in long, smooth strokes, brushing her golden hair into soft waves. When no snarls remained, she gathered it back from either side of her face, twisted it into a knot at the nape of her neck, and fastened it in place with a pair of carved wooden combs. She picked up

17

the little gold ring featuring two clasped hands that had been her mother's and slipped it over the knuckle of her third finger. Pressing a quick kiss to it in honor of the mother she never knew, she slipped into her well-worn cloak and headed out the door.

* * *

As the door closed behind Veronika, anxious words burst from Jana's lips. "Oh, Antonin, what's to become of her? We won't be living forever to look out for her. She needs a husband, I'm thinking. And it's for certain she deserves one that'll look well to caring for her—her being so good and dear. That Boris up the street keeps hanging round, drooling over her like a starving dog," she made a wry face, "but I'm right glad she doesn't seem to pay him any mind."

Antonin's startled expression made the plump little woman hastily qualify, "Oh, I'm not being proud with Boris; he is our neighbor and all." She threw out her work-worn hands in frustration and bemoaned, "But he's got no prospects that I can tell. And he doesn't seem to have a mind to look for any, either."

Tears welled up in her eyes and overflowed into all the little creases time had etched in her face. Her voice fell to a whisper, "It's just that I want more for

Veronika—I want her to be well cared for and to find the happiness we've shared." Jana lowered her head and began to cry, uncharacteristically distraught.

Antonin shuffled over to his weeping wife, tugged her into his arms, and held her tightly to his heart. "There, there," he whispered, gently smoothing his hand over her silvered hair to the bun at the back of her head. "We must be finding our trust in our Heavenly Father. He'll be providing for our dear girl whatever seems best to Him. He's been faithful all along; I doubt He'll decide to be stopping now. So don't you be fretting yourself."

He helped her over to a chair and fussed about her lovingly. "You'll just be making yourself sick— and all for nothing, you'll be seeing."

"I'm knowing you're right," the old woman sniffled, impatiently brushing away her tears with twisted, gnarled fingers, "but will you be speaking a prayer with me anyhow?" They clasped their hands together like two trusting children and asked their faithful Father to care for their precious girl.

* * *

At The Three Claws Inn, not far from Hana's corner bakery where Veronika had stopped to buy

19

the jam-filled buns, Lord Nick and Lady Kitty Branden, along with their son David and daughter Lucina, sat around the small table in the larger of their two rented rooms.

The sumptuous evening meal, in keeping with the reputation of The Three Claws Inn, consisted of four rye bread trenchers, each cradling a roasted pheasant basted to a golden brown and seasoned with butter, salt, and rosemary; a medley of boiled potatoes, carrots, and leeks; and a baked apple, cut open and garnished with a drizzle of honey and a sprinkle of cloves, a rare and costly spice. A platter displaying a round of aged cheese and a stone crock filled with sliced, fermented cabbage sat in the middle of the table, along with the pastries procured by Lady Branden and Lucina from Hana's bakery. A pitcher of sweet cider rounded out the meal.

The elegant establishment boasted King Zikmund's patronage during his several past visits to Prague and offered spacious rooms with daily maid service to empty chamber pots and deliver coal in cold weather. Guests enjoyed two meals each day— eaten in the great hall with other guests or in the privacy of a personal chamber, along with the luxury of hot water in a copper tub for a once-a-week bath. Lord Branden had procured the inn's two largest rooms for their week-long stay.

The Brandens had brought David to enroll in Charles University, Lord Branden's alma mater. Including his wife and daughter on this trip fulfilled a promise Lord Branden had made to his wife before they were married, to someday take her to Prague to see the famed astronomical clock that he said was reputed to be one of only three in the world, the magnificent Stone Bridge spanning the golden Vlatava River, St. George's Basilica with its twin spires, and St. Vitus's Cathedral—ever a work in progress.

Now that she had seen the city where her son would live for the next two years, Lady Branden felt reconciled to leaving him.

Lord Branden had investigated housing arrangements, giving careful thought to the options available to David, which included living with a family, renting a single room in a house or hotel, or renting a room in a boarding house. Lord Branden finally decided on the large upstairs room in At the Stone Swan, concluding that a boarding house's meals and laundry service along with limited independence would be good for David's first venture away from home.

Once their son was established, the Brandens would begin the long journey back to Burg Mosel, their ancestral home.

After a hotel maid cleared away the remains of the evening meal, Lord Branden left the hotel and went for a walk. David brought out his inlaid ivory and ebony chessboard and placed it on the table. Lucina, who was still learning the finer points of the game, began arranging the chess pieces. Lady Branden collected her needlework and settled in a chair by the candle stand.

With imminent separation from her son topmost in her mind, Lady Branden's concern for David's spiritual life prompted her to comment with as much diplomacy as she could manage, "Lucina and I stopped at a little bakery in Celetna Street on our way back to the inn—that's where I bought the pastries we ate tonight. While we were in the shop, the clerk's daughter asked a customer, a young woman, if she would be attending "Fellowship" tonight. I wondered what she meant, so after the customer left, I visited with the proprietor.

"She told me that small church home groups called United Fellowships meet weekly all over the city, and anyone is welcome to attend. I asked for the directions to their group, David. I thought you might like to go. They meet every Thursday evening."

Observing David's raised eyebrow that betrayed his annoyance, Lady Branden defended her suggestion. "Just consider it, Son; that's all I ask."

Somehow, in spite of everything she'd done to encourage David's faith, her son had shown little interest in spiritual things. Her husband said not to worry, the boy would grow in faith as he matured, but she feared they had spoiled him. Oh, it wasn't that he'd ever done anything bad. It was just that his life had been filled with parental love and social privilege, and he'd yet to become aware of his need for God.

Lucina was a different story. It seemed she'd been born loving God. A serious little soul, among her first sentences was, "We pray?" She'd been Lady Branden's comfort and joy in the four years since the death of her mother-in-law, Lady Rosamund.

When David didn't reply, Lady Branden dropped the subject, heaving an inward sigh. She'd have to trust God to help her son see his need. Nagging or lecturing would only drive him away from her—and from God.

CHAPTER TWO

Friday morning started early for Veronika. To be sure, her usual rising time of four-thirty felt early every morning, but attending Fellowship made her Thursday night bedtime later than usual, cutting short her rest and making her feel like sleep had hardly come before it had to be left behind in the warmth of her narrow bed.

Hurrying across the Stone Bridge, Veronika couldn't help noticing dawn's faint golden light reflecting off the gentle ripples on the surface of the quietly flowing Vltava River. She sniffed the air with pleasure at the smell of ripening apples from an orchard up-river and hugged her arms tightly around her middle for protection against the early morning chill.

As the sun rose over the horizon, promising a sunny autumn day, she dashed the last few steps and arrived at the servants' entrance of At the Stone Swan with only a few minutes to spare.

Miss Hesta, the older woman who managed the household's daily operations, was waiting for her at the door.

"Good morning," Veronika greeted politely, stepping inside. She suppressed a shiver as her body adjusted to the warmer temperature in the boarding house.

She couldn't help but notice that Miss Hesta was clutching a valuable gray-green glass vase to her chest, but she knew better than to comment on something outside her responsibility; Miss Hesta disliked nosy busybodies.

While Veronika removed her cloak and hat and hung them on her assigned peg, Miss Hesta outlined the maid's morning assignment. "A new boarder is arriving today . . . a university student named Mr. Branden. He's taking the large room at the top of the stairs."

Miss Hesta, who gestured wildly with her hands when she spoke, waved the flute-necked vessel in the air. "Hurry now. Get the room ready before you see to your other duties."

"Yes, Miss Hesta." In spite of her gruff manner, the house manager was a good-hearted soul who knew that making a new boarder's room pleasant and welcoming rated as Veronika's favorite task.

As Veronika fastened her white head covering in place, Miss Hesta turned to go then swung back around. "Oh, and hurry to the garden and cut some roses." She thrust the vase toward the maid. "Madam said to fill this vase with roses and put it in the new boarder's window."

Veronika couldn't stop her mouth from gaping. They'd never put flowers in any boarder's room, and besides, the weather had turned so cold she wasn't sure there would be any flowers left to cut.

As Miss Hesta finished her explanation, she flung her hands in the air in a gesture of surrender. "Mr. Branden's family will be coming with him. Since Widow Flek is charging a dear price for that room, she wants it to look like it's worth the cost. She said mothers always notice things like flowers."

* * *

Veronika stood in the doorway of the soon-to-be-occupied upstairs room. She'd lugged a bucket heaped with coal chunks up the stairs, taking care not to bang her shins, and emptied them into the ceramic stove. The fire now blazing in it had chased away the chill. After draping the duvet out the window and beating it with a wooden paddle to fluff the feathers, she'd added several handfuls of dried lavender buds to the feathers to freshen their stale odor and then re-made the bed. A plump, brown cushion now padded the seat of the room's solitary chair, and a round, braided rug in browns and greens warmed the wood floor.

Veronika smiled and nodded to herself. She knew she'd done a good job. Indeed, the room reflected her touch; it was clean, bright, and cheerful. The room stood ready for the new boarder.

That is, except for the roses.

Moving toward the window, Veronika carried the green vase filled with water in one hand and gingerly clutched an assortment of aromatic, prickly-stemmed roses in the other. She'd cut the few full blooms that remained. After settling the vase on the wide ledge at the base of the leaded, paned window, she began poking the stems into the water.

Voices in the garden below snagged Veronika's attention. As she leaned close to look out the window, a thrill of surprise made her catch her breath. Widow Flek was speaking with the beautiful woman she'd seen yesterday in Hana's bakery! And the young girl, Lucina, stood close to her mother and held her hand.

After a moment, her gaze took in a broad shouldered young man and a handsome older gentleman approaching from around the side of the boarding house. The young man, who looked to be about Veronika's own age, mirrored the older man's noble bearing and dark good looks. Her heart gave a funny little twist; the young man looked exactly like the prince of her imagination in her favorite childhood folktale, *Bella Venezia.*

"Who are these people, and what are they doing here?" she muttered to herself, drawing in the scent of the roses as she leaned over the vase.

And then it struck her. They were the Brandens. And that handsome young man was At the Stone Swan's new boarder!

As if she'd seen a ghost, Veronika jerked her head back from the window. Oh, whatever was she doing, dawdling in *his* room? She didn't want to be found here, and certainly not at the task of arranging flowers for him!

She looked down with a grimace—this apron had to be her shabbiest.

Frantically, she jammed the last rose stem into the vase and winced when a thorn pricked her finger. The wound stung like a physical reflection of her conscience, smarting over her vanity.

But there was no time to think about that now.

In the next moment, Veronika went flying down the stairs, nursing the gouge in her finger between her lips.

Safely inside the servants' quarters, she closed the door and sagged against it. And just in time, too. Voices in the hall told her that the Branden family had entered the house.

Wiping her hand over her face, Veronika chided herself, "You are a foolish girl. As if the Brandens will even notice you, a housemaid, much less care what you look like." Nevertheless, she removed her head covering, smoothed her hair, and refastened the triangular scarf beneath her hair at the back of her neck before she collected a bucket of coal and lugged it into the parlor. As she scuttled the lumps into the chute, she held her breath because breathing in the lignite dust always made her sneeze.

Miss Merta, one of the other maids, poked her head around the corner and said in a loud whisper,

"Miss V'ronika, d'ja get n'eyeful of our new boarder?" Miss Merta's speech betrayed her country roots. "His ol' man's a lord. An' 'is mam . . ." the maid rolled her eyes exaggeratedly instead of finishing her sentence. "An' d'ja evah see sech a fur cloak . . ? Why, the price of it'd be keepin' me fer life."

Veronika clenched her teeth and slowly released her breath through them. Although she refused to make a caustic reply, she didn't want to listen to Miss Merta—or anybody else—speak frivolously about the lady she so admired. She deliberately fixed her eyes on the bucket as the last of the coal tumbled into the chute.

* * *

Miss Merta scurried away, shaking her head as she mused, *That Miss V'ronika's a hard one ta be figgerin'. However can she be happy an' contentioned when she's missin' the 'citement of bein' young an' makin' the mos' uh life's chancees?*

Aftah all, I'm notta thinkin' ta be somebody's maid fer all me life. Why, if I 'pply me wits, this han'some new gent'man could be the one ta savior me. Or I might even be findin' the luck ta be Lady Somethin'-er-othah. You jes' nevah can be knowin'.

Too bad Miss V'ronika nevah takes no int'rest in any ah the boarders. But 'er lack ah int'rest is makin' the comp'tition a mitle more easy, since she's the far prettliest maid . . .

The house manager's sharp hand-clap and reprimand broke into her fantasy. "Miss Merta, quit your daydreaming and get to work."

"Yes, Miss Hesta." Merta sighed again. *Oh, ta be a mos' wondrus lady, orderin' others ta do these horridous tasks!*

* * *

"Miss Veronika?" Miss Hesta's gruff voice echoed in the stairwell as she descended the steps. "Come here at once."

"Yes, Miss Hesta. At your service," Veronika answered respectfully, emerging around the corner from the parlor.

"When Lady Branden admired the roses you put in the window, Widow Flek said she'd give her a bush for her garden. Be off with you now; fetch a shovel from the shed and dig up one." The house manager made a scuttling gesture toward the door.

Veronika raised her finely arched brows in surprise. "Which one?"

Miss Hesta threw her hands out and shook them impatiently. "Oh, it doesn't matter—just pick one. And leave plenty of dirt around the roots. I've never heard of such a thing, but we just do as we're told. Put it in an empty water pail and bring it round front. Hurry, now. They'll be taking their leave soon."

Veronika dashed to the kitchen to collect her cloak and a water pail and then ran to the shed. Her pounding heart constricted her breathing.

A rose bush for the beautiful lady. Lady Branden.

At the edge of the garden, Veronika dropped the pail and grasped the shovel handle with both hands. Wide-eyed, she scanned the bushes. Which one? Oh, how was she to decide which rose would please Lady Branden? Since the blooms were gone, there was no way to know the flower color of each bush. She felt beads of perspiration pop out on her forehead. Then her gaze landed on a small bush near the back of the garden that was sheltered from the wind by several tall trees. A closer look revealed two dainty, yellow, almost-open buds. Yes, this one would be just right.

Veronika repeatedly plunged the shovel into the cold ground around the bush to loosen the soil. When the root ball was finally free, she left it in the hole and dropped the shovel. She grabbed the pail handle and plopped it down beside the bush. Taking up the shovel again, she thrust the blade under the root ball, pressed her lips together, and heaved with all her strength. Slowly, the bush erupted out of the sandy earth. She balanced it on the blade and moved it to the pail. As the root ball sank into the empty container, loose soil cascaded over the rim. She dropped the shovel and grasped the pail handle. Straining against the weight of the filled bucket, she moved it aside.

When a dribble of perspiration tickled Veronika's cheek, she instinctively brushed at the moisture with the back of her hand. Gulping in a deep, fortifying breath of air that held nuances of sandy soil and fallen leaves, she grasped the shovel handle with both hands and scraped the loose dirt back into the hole. To even out the ground, she pared soil from the surrounding area and scraped it into the hole. With the backside of the shovel blade, she tamped it down and then scraped more soil to the sunken spot until the ground was even.

Satisfied that she'd done her best to repair the hole, Veronika ran to the shed to return the shovel and then raced back to the garden to collect the rose bush. The pail's weight strained her arms in their sockets, and she tried not to stagger as she lugged the pail across the yard.

Veronika rounded the corner of the boarding house in time to see Widow Flek's stout figure proceed through the front door. Her hearty voice boomed, "Oh, there you are, Missy. Set the pail here." She pointed to a spot on the ground a mere two paces in front of her.

Veronika quickly did as she was told, hoping to escape without being seen in such an overheated state. But as she straightened up, Lady Branden appeared in the doorway.

"Your rose bush," Widow Flek said, her decisive nod in Veronika's direction sending her guest's attention to the pail resting on the ground in front of Veronika.

Observing the tiny yellow buds, Lady Branden raised startled green eyes to Veronika's face. "Oh, *Dívčí*, how did you know that yellow roses are my favorite?"

The mellow voice held pleasure and something else; it was as if the woman knew her. Of course, they had both been in Hana's bakeshop, Veronika mused; that must be it. She tried not to stare. The woman was lovelier than she remembered—and exuded a musky, exotic scent.

Dropping a curtsey, Veronika stammered in a nervous rush, "Oh. Why, I'm sure I didn't, my lady, but when I went to dig up a bush, this one seemed right for you."

"Nonsense, Child," Widow Flek snapped impatiently, "I wouldn't want Lady Branden thinking you have magical powers." Then as if realizing she sounded harsh, she added, "But you did make a good choice." She dismissed Veronika with an impatient wave of her fleshy hand and returned her focus to her impressive visitor.

* * *

Excited to be independent and ready for adventure, David Branden said goodbye to his family at the doorway of his spacious new room. But when a wave of melancholy overcame him at the last minute; he dashed across the hall to the open window and looked down on the street below.

Arriving in time to view and hear the interchange between his departing mother and the dainty maid, he abruptly drew back. The maid had chosen a yellow rose bush for his mother!

He stiffened his jaw. His mother would say the maid's choice was significant. He would say it was foolish—nothing more than female superstition.

A yellow rose may have held a special place in the romantic history of his family, but a serious interest in some lowly housemaid had no place in his life right now. This new university adventure, filled with friends, noise, and activity, promised to be too exciting to miss.

The more serious things in life would just have to wait.

CHAPTER THREE

One year later.

"David, would you care to join my family for dinner on Tuesday evening?" Professor Martin Bortskova, the mentor assigned by the university to work with David in overseeing his second year of education, had also been his father's mentor. For this reason, the older gentleman took an exceptional interest in him.

"Yes, I'd be pleased to come." David felt a thrill of excitement to be singled out for favor by one of the university's most popular professors.

On the set date, David met Professor Bortskova after his last class and accompanied him home from the university. As they walked toward the professor's residence, located a dozen streets away from the university in the opposite direction from At The Stone Swan, the older man spoke about his family.

"When my wife died eight years ago, I found it difficult to live alone, so I invited my son Richard, his wife, Irena, and my granddaughter, Rayna, who was nine years old at the time, to share my home. They've lived with me for the past seven years."

While they were still at a distance, the professor pointed out his home. In contrast to the narrow, pinched faces of the row houses filling the city, the large dwelling stood on a grassy knoll surrounded on three sides by mature walnut trees. The structure's weathered stones were all faded to the same dull shade of gray. Thick ivy covered one end of the house, grew up the massive chimney, and climbed over part of the roof. Bits of color—yellow, orange, purple, and white—provided by late-blooming asters and calendula, clung to the lower edge of the house.

David's anticipation increased with each step. If the grounds were any indication of the warmth and care awaiting him inside, the evening just might assuage the dull ache of missing his family.

A broad flagstone supporting gleaming copper pots filled with aromatic purple lavender provided a friendly welcome at the front door, but when David followed his mentor inside, he stopped abruptly. The foyer was dark and spare, not at all inviting, as the outside implied.

Professor Bortskova, catching the puzzled expression on his young guest's face, hastened to explain, "Irena is a good woman but, ah, very practical. When my Sarka was alive, the house was warm and welcoming. But I don't mind. Irena means well." He shrugged. "I take care of the outside."

David hooked his winter garments on one of the pegs above the long entry bench and drew in a slow, savoring breath. The aroma of herbs and spices was enough to make him forget everything except how much he was looking forward to a meal prepared with palate pleasure in mind. Two meals a day kept the boarding house residents alive; however, they definitely lacked the mark of a cook whose goal was to make food a satisfying experience for the soul as well as the body.

Breakfast each morning consisted of porridge and black rye bread with creamy cheese, accompanied by jam or nut spread. The evening meal was usually cabbage soup or a root vegetable stew with venison, always accompanied by apples, rye bread, and hard cheese.

David followed Martin into the dining room and acknowledged the professor's brief introductions before he joined the family around the table. After a recited grace offered by his host, a man-servant filled each person's goblet. A maid in a cap and apron placed a pewter charger holding a trencher of crusty bread in front of each diner.

A roasted game hen surrounded by mushrooms, chopped turnips, and apples, all drizzled with a currant and honey glaze, filled the trencher and was enough to make David's mouth water—and the presentation alone compensated for any lack in his hostess's ability to infuse a house with warmth.

Although Richard spoke no more than six words the entire evening, his wife made up for him, maintaining a steady stream of advice, opinions, and questions for each person around the table. David obligingly answered those she directed to him: Where did he come from? What was his father's occupation? How much property belonged to his father's estate? Was his father titled? Did he have siblings or was he the sole heir?

David chuckled under his breath; Irena forthrightly extracted the state of his father's fortune while her reticent husband, Richard, nodded approvingly at his replies.

When he'd reduced his partridge to bones with the help of his personal, finely-crafted silver knife, a going-to-university gift from his parents, Irena prompted the maid to offer him a second portion. Irena liked him—or his knife, he decided, amused by that notion. Everyone carried their personal eating utensil, but his was the work of a master silversmith, and several times during the meal he'd noted Irena covertly studying it.

Professor Bortskova's granddaughter, Rayna, smiled nervously and blushed every time he glanced her way. She was slant-shouldered and rather plain, and her crooked teeth triggered the contrasting image of the maid Veronika's even, pearly smile, but a rapid blink of his eyes quickly erased that unbidden thought. However, because Rayna seemed to spend more time watching him than eating, by mid-meal he avoided looking in her direction.

David's decision to ignore the Spartan setting and exert his charm paid off. As he swung his cloak around and rested it on his shoulders, preparing to depart, Irena surprised him by inviting him to join them for dinner every Sunday night. He agreed with sincere enthusiasm; dining at the Bortskova home once each week would provide a gratifying alternative to the boarding house's simple meals.

After that first evening, David found himself looking forward to his weekly visit with the Bortskova family. In fact, it became his personal challenge to make the intense, thin-faced Irena smile at least once each evening. And he usually succeeded. And while the visits didn't eliminate his occasional longing for home, they did provide a pleasant variation to boarding house fare.

His living situation, however, proved better than he'd expected. The nine boarders of At The Stone Swan, each a male university student, proved a friendly lot, and the harpsichord in the parlor, an unexpected luxury, provided him an easy connection with them. Often in the evenings they would gather around him to sing folk ballads, make up their own ditties, or listen to him play.

Widow Flek always greeted him by name. Since he paid considerably more rent than the other boarders, particularly those who shared a room that was much smaller than his, he knew it was good business on her part to treat him well. But he also knew he could be charming, so each time they met he made a point to compliment her on some aspect of her establishment.

The maids went out of their way to be pleasant, and their obvious attention made daily life easy. Well, actually, all the maids were friendly except Miss Veronika. To be honest, it galled him that even now, after almost a year of boarding, she remained aloof— no matter how cheerfully he greeted her. She was by far the most lady-like and the most attractive, and he had to admit he respected her for not fawning over him or the other young men who were his fellow boarders. Not even when she had the opportunity.

Like this morning.

He'd raced back to the boarding house in the late morning to collect a forgotten lesson exercise, intending to slip in and out unnoticed. Just thinking about it made him chuckle; he usually enjoyed attracting attention.

He knew, in a vague way, that someone emptied his stove and filled the pail with coal in the winter, refilled his water pitcher every day, and put fresh seasonal flowers in his window. Because he never happened to be around when all that took place, he'd given it little thought.

But this morning, as he neared the top of the stairs he saw that the heavy door he'd closed when he left now stood open. He could hear someone in his room softly singing a lilting melody.

Curiosity piqued, David tiptoed up the last three steps.

Surprise brought him to a halt in the doorway. Silhouetted against the many-paned window, Miss Veronika stood with her head bent over a slender vase, her nose buried in the single rose it held. Yes, it was a yellow rose.

And what a picture she made. His pulse rate accelerated as the pretty maid and her whimsical song captivated his imagination. Unexpected thoughts flashed through his mind—thoughts of tenderness and longing.

Veronika lifted her head. When she saw David in the doorway, her voice died in her throat. She gasped and flushed. Swallowing hard, she finally stammered out an awkward apology, "I-I'm so s-sorry. I'm not q-quite finished here."

Before he had a chance to reply, Veronika's eyes darted to the duvet hanging out the window for its morning airing. "I'll put the—the—I'll come back later." Her blush receded, leaving her ghostly pale—and making David wish he could read her mind.

Veronika moved toward the door, obviously intending to escape. "Please, excuse me," she whispered, avoiding his eyes.

Instead of stepping aside, David reached boldly across the open doorway. As his hand grasped the doorframe, his extended arm deliberately blocked her exit. "Look at me," he commanded. "I want to talk to you."

Veronika's brown eyes, dark pools of mute entreaty, met his blue ones.

Ignoring her silent plea, he confronted her directly. "You avoid me, Miss Veronika. Why? What have I done to offend you?"

"Ah, y-you haven't d-done anything. It's just that the other maids . . ." She clamped her lips shut on the rest of the sentence.

"What about the other maids?" His quizzical expression nearly stopped her heart.

"Please," she begged, desperation oozing through her words, "I didn't mean anything."

He nonchalantly rested his broad shoulder against the door frame. "But of course you did. And I want to know, what about the others?" His tone held an element of demand.

Veronika gulped. And gulped again. How could this be happening?

"I'm waiting." David raised one dark eyebrow expectantly.

Veronika clenched her hands into fists. The muscles tightened in her throat. Perspiration popped out on her brow and her voice came out low and miserable. "It's just that . . ." A groan suffocated her words.

"Yes?" he prompted.

She finally mumbled, "Th-the other maids think you're . . . charming and . . ." She flushed and averted her gaze.

"And?"

". . . and handsome . . ." She glanced up to look at him and found herself trapped by a pair of intense blue eyes.

". . . and wealthy . . ." Her voice trembled and died of embarrassment.

"And?" he prompted again. Was that a twinkle lurking in his eyes?

". . . and they . . ."

His lips twitched; there was no question he was fighting a grin.

Goaded beyond mortification, she snapped, "You know very well they would all like to be your wife!"

After a moment of stunned surprise, David threw back his head and laughed. "They would, would they?" He slanted her a teasing look. "All of them at once, I suppose."

Veronika's eyes flashed, and he saw that she almost laughed with him; it did sound foolish when said out loud.

Quick to take advantage of her momentary vulnerability, David cocked his head and baited, "So, I take it you don't agree with them?"

Veronika's mouth sagged open.

David straightened up and took several bold steps toward her. "Well, the least you could do is act friendly. I'm not an ogre, you know."

Desperate to end her humiliation, Veronika pushed past him and ran down the stairs.

He stared after her. Yellow roses, indeed.

* * *

There must be a way out of this predicament, Veronika feverishly prodded her tortured mind as she trudged over the Stone Bridge on her way home. David Branden's appearance in the doorway of his room this morning precisely when she'd been thinking about him was positively uncanny. It was a good thing he wasn't able to hear her thoughts. Her cheeks grew warm, just thinking about it.

For months she'd disciplined herself to consider Widow Flek's captivating boarder in no other terms than simply someone to be served, but the hurt in his voice when he'd accused her of ignoring him had taken her by surprise. She'd thought he wouldn't notice her remoteness because he was continually surrounded by friends and activity. Besides, her status as a servant didn't exactly put her in his social sphere.

Veronika was determined to value character over appearance, but David's innate charm haunted her, and sometimes she found herself watching him surreptitiously from the edges of boarding house activity.

She'd noticed small things. He wiped his hand over his face when thinking hard. And lifted one eyebrow when he was amused or annoyed. He had an easy stride—with his shoulders squared and his head high. A far-away expression settled over his countenance when his long fingers coaxed music from the harpsichord in the parlor. And his warm, rumbling laugh was infectious; it sent shivers from her head to her toes.

She'd wanted to die when he demanded she finish her incriminating sentence. She'd betrayed the other maids, and she couldn't talk to them about it—that would make matters worse for everyone. And if she started treating David in a friendly fashion, he might conclude that she agreed with the other maids' matrimonial longings.

Dear God, how had she become entangled in this tricky situation? And more important, how could she get out of it? If she said or did anything to make things worse, she could lose her job. She would just have to avoid him. And when that wasn't possible, she would be cordial. But nothing more.

* * *

Five days later, Veronika secretly congratulated herself on her resolution—which seemed to be working. She'd successfully avoided David and even managed to trade the daily care of his room with Miss Merta by offering to fill the other maid's coal buckets each day from the mountain of sooty chunks in the coal bin—a messy job that Miss Merta despised.

51

But Veronika's success was short-lived.

On Thursday evening, just like every Thursday evening, Veronika's childhood friend, Helina Marenkova, and her older brother, Boris, walked down the hill, passing the four houses located between their homes, and stopped at the Karska's humble dwelling so they could walk together to Fellowship.

Although they had played together often when they were children, now that Veronika and Helina were grown, long work-days filled most of their time. Veronika supported herself as well as Antonin and Jana Karska, while Helina contributed to her family's income, which was particularly needful since Boris was socially awkward and had a hard time keeping a job. Both girls looked forward to their weekly Thursday walk to and from Fellowship because it kept them connected.

When the knocker clattered, Veronika promptly joined them. The fading daylight shadowed their faces, emphasizing their thick brown hair, strong cheekbones, and deeply set eyes framed by heavy brows that almost met in the middle. No one would mistake their family resemblance; they looked enough alike to be twins.

Helina hooked her arm through Veronika's and began chattering as the two young women proceeded down the middle of the narrow, cobbled street to avoid the occasional deluge of foul water tossed out of an upper story window. Tall and broad-chested, with a thick neck and brooding demeanor, Boris tagged along behind them.

As they crossed the bridge, Boris, who had a habit of invading people's personal space, walked too close to Veronika and bumped into her from behind, causing her to stumble. Instantly, he grabbed her arms to steady her, his strong hands squeezing until it hurt.

When she could manage to speak without betraying her discomfort, Veronika reassured him kindly, "I'm quite alright, Boris."

They set off again, Veronika trying not to wince at the pain in her arms. She felt certain Boris had not meant her harm; he just did not realize his strength.

A few steps later, Boris bumped into her again.

This time, Veronika turned her head to look up at him and found him so close that her hair brushed his sleeve.

Before she had time to suggest that he step back a bit, he said, "You smell good."

Speechless, Veronika finally produced a half-chuckle. "Oh, thank you, but could you not walk so close?" She was grateful he hadn't grabbed her again.

During the remainder of the twenty-minute walk to the Jamikovi's home, Boris interrupted the girls several times to ask Veronika in three- or four-word sentences about her work and about the boarders she served. Because Boris rarely spoke, Veronika thought his interest seemed out of character, but she concluded that perhaps it was his way of apologizing. However, when he suggested he could wait every day at the boarding house for her to get off work so he could walk her home, she felt decidedly uncomfortable.

Helina was her valued friend, and Veronika understood her protectiveness of her brother's deficiencies, so once again she chose to be gracious.

"Oh, Boris, that's very thoughtful of you, but you might find a job in the next day or two, and then you wouldn't want to be committed to waiting for me." She sincerely hoped her diplomacy would put him off his idea.

Boris grunted, then persisted. "But I might not. Find a job, that is. And you need me. I'm strong. I can keep you safe."

This time Veronika's tone was more serious. "There's really no need. I've been coming and going on my own for three years."

"But you might get hurt. I could protect you."

"A-ahh . . ." Veronika stammered. How could she convince him to drop his idea without hurting his feelings?

Helina solved the problem for her, scolding him as only a sister can do. "Boris! Leave Veronika alone. She just said she doesn't need any help."

Boris growled something Veronika didn't quite catch, but his peculiar interest in her affairs seemed entirely too personal. She suppressed a shudder and was glad when they reached the towering poplar trees that marked the Jamikovi's property boundary.

They walked along the large building that housed Lucas's wagon, cart, and carriage building company. Lucas had inherited the business from his father, but it was his skill as a craftsman and good business sense that had built it into a booming enterprise.

Just beyond the workshop, light shone out of the windows of the Jamikovi's two-story stone-and-mortar home and blanketed Eva's extensive herb garden in a soft glow. The scents of sage, lavender, basil, and mint tickled their noses as they passed by. They followed the flagstone path to the front door, where Eva welcomed them into her spacious entry hall.

"I'll take your things," she offered as they shed their winter wraps. "Go on in and find a place to sit. Tomas and Milan are already here. Lucas will be out in a minute; he's just washing up."

Boris and Helina, both taller and sturdier than Veronika, preceded her through the doorway, blocking her view into the parlor. When Boris immediately dropped into a tall-backed chair near the door, Veronika felt some of the tension leave her body; his strange behavior earlier had made her worry that he would insist on sitting beside her.

Helina moved out of Veronika's line of sight, claiming a vacant space between Tomas and Milan, two middle-aged widowers seated on the long, padded settee. That left Veronika gazing across the room, directly into David Branden's sky-blue eyes.

Her breath caught in her throat. What was he doing here? Her frustration with Boris was instantly swallowed up in fear that she would reveal the attraction she felt for David.

Upon seeing her, David's expression changed from surprise to something she couldn't quite identify. And when he patted the chair next to his and invited, "Here's an empty seat," heat suffused her body, flooding her with an overwhelming urge to turn and run.

But not for anything, she decided, would she give that smug young man such satisfaction. She steeled her nerves against her anxiety, forced her face into a cool smile, and made a brave effort to nonchalantly slip into the chair he'd indicated. Snagging a loose curl, she looped it behind her ear in a deliberately carefree gesture and sternly reminded herself that in David's eyes she was a lowly housemaid—and she would do well not to forget it.

When she'd settled, David leaned toward her and bent his head to whisper near her ear, "I'm surprised to see you here. But I guess I shouldn't be. It all fits."

His warm breath on her cheek along with his puzzling comment made her shift uneasily in her seat. "Wha-what fits?" she stammered. This was certainly not a direction she'd anticipated a conversation with David taking!

"You. Here. At a prayer meeting."

She felt herself stiffen. "Why should that surprise you?" She tried not to sound defensive, but she knew she did.

"It shouldn't surprise me," he stated without emotion as he leaned back in his chair and studied her curiously. "In fact, it's just what I should have expected . . . to find you here. A girl who would give my mother a *yellow* rose bush would be the kind of girl to go to a prayer meeting."

"That was over a year ago!" Veronika's astonishment gave way to suspicion; she might be naive but this was a ploy if she'd ever heard one. "Besides, what's the color of roses got to do with me going to a prayer meeting?" she sniped, abandoning her intention to remain cool and detached.

"Wouldn't you like to know!" he baited, his face alive with an endearingly mischievous grin that made her break out in a cold sweat.

She dragged her gaze away from his dancing eyes. "Not really," she said, striving for disdain.

David was silent so long she couldn't help stealing a glance at him. And found him staring at her.

"You should," he said enigmatically, cocking his head and quirking one dark eyebrow.

Her mind went blank; she couldn't think of a single clever retort. Would she ever understand how men think? Really, two bizarre conversations in one evening were more than she could handle!

She tore her eyes away from David, only to meet the reproachful gaze of Boris, glaring at her from across the room. Her heart sank; she would no doubt have to deal with him again on the way home.

"Good evening, good evening," Lucas greeted as he followed Eva into the parlor, bringing with him the smell of lye soap—the result of his effort to rid his hands of grease and wood resin.

Distracted by their host's greeting, Boris broke eye contact. Relieved for the moment, Veronika quickly shifted her attention to Lucas. As she focused on his face, the thought struck her that she'd never before noticed how his large ears stuck straight out from his head.

Instantly horrified at her shallow criticism, she corrected herself. Lucas couldn't help what his ears looked like; he was a good man and a faithful Believer. Oh, whatever was the matter with her?

Suddenly the sound of David's voice jerked Veronika's mind back to the present, ". . . and that's how I knew about your meeting." She stared at the floor and pursed her lips. Most certainly, she would like to know just how David Branden knew about their Fellowship meetings.

In the next moment, disgusted with herself for feeling irritated, Veronika set her mind to ignore both disturbing young men. She wasn't about to let either of them spoil the evening for her when it was her only social interaction and the highlight of her week.

But her good intentions went unfulfilled. Before she knew it, the meeting was over and she couldn't recall singing a single song or anything anyone had said.

Veronika put her head down to avoid being pulled into conversation and rushed into the guest room opening off the foyer, where she frantically rifled through the assortment of winter garments heaped on the bed until she found her own. With her belongings clutched in her arms, she darted into the dimly lit entry hall, anxious to be out the door.

After she'd hurriedly wrapped herself in her cloak and tied the cords to her hat under her chin, she shifted restlessly from one foot to the other. For her own safety, she knew she should wait for Boris and

Helina to finish visiting. But oh, how she wanted to dash out the door and run all the way home.

Finally, feeling too warm bundled in her winter garments, she put her hand on the door latch, intending to step outside.

Just then, David rushed into the foyer. "Veronika, wait," he called, swinging his cloak around his shoulders as he hurried up to her.

Veronika looked at him and almost laughed; in his haste he'd plopped his fur hat on his head at a skewed angle. But when he reached for her arm and said, "Come, I'll walk you home," she stiffened and clenched her hands into fists. Her mind raced frantically. How could she get out of it?

"Oh, I'm so sorry." Dropping her chin to hide the flush of her repressed emotions, Veronika muttered softly for his ears only, "I'm with Boris, and he'll expect me to go back with him." Maybe a feigned former commitment would put David off without antagonizing him. She had no reason to expect him to be any different than the other wealthy university young men through the years who'd sought to warm their beds with a house maid. Believing David's interest to be sincere was exactly what she cautioned all the maids she trained to guard against.

Intent on their conversation, neither of them noticed Boris round the corner behind Veronika. Overhearing David's invitation and Veronika's declaration, Boris suddenly moved forward and gripped her shoulders with possessive hands, pulling her back against his chest. He glared at David, his chin jutting and his proprietary tone laced with a threatening undercurrent. "She's with me, Branden."

Veronika jerked around, gasping as dismay sent her heart plummeting to her feet. Why, oh, why did Boris have to appear at precisely the wrong moment? He had made the situation a hundred times worse!

As Boris tightened his grip, Veronika found herself unable to speak.

"Fine," David said, raising his dark brows over narrowed eyes. He shrugged, opened the door, and walked out of the house without a backward glance.

Veronika stared blankly at the door as it slammed shut, and Boris loudly cleared his throat twice before she regained her presence of mind. As she pulled away from him, Helina and the two widowers entered the foyer. Relief made Veronika's legs go weak; she'd been rescued—at least for the present moment!

Anxious to get home before the ten o'clock city curfew landed them in jail, everyone moved out the door and headed their separate ways. Boris didn't say anything about what had transpired earlier, and Veronika didn't know what to say that wouldn't humiliate him in front of his sister. She trudged along in silent agony, her eyes riveted on her shoes that felt as heavy as if their soles were made of lead. It required all her strength to pick up her feet so as not to stub her toes on the uneven cobbles obscured by the darkness.

Added to her frustration, guilt and shame tortured her conscience. She'd always prided herself on her honesty—and now look what she'd done; she'd as good as told David Branden there was more than just a friendship between Boris and her.

To make matters worse, Boris had overheard her exaggeration of the truth. Although he'd always acted in a mildly possessive manner, she'd thought it was because she was his sister's friend. But how could she tell him that his behavior tonight had gone beyond mild?

And as hard as she tried, she could not imagine confessing to David that there was no relationship beyond friendship between Boris and her. Or that she'd been deliberately dishonest in using Boris as an excuse to avoid walking home with him. Oh, what a mess she had gotten herself into.

Ever the more loquacious of the two friends, Helina chattered away as usual, seemingly content with Veronika's minimal responses. Then just before the threesome reached the Karska's home, Helina brought up the subject that had disturbed Veronika earlier in the evening.

"Wasn't it great how Mr. Branden's mother wrote to remind him about our Fellowship meetings? I wonder who she overheard in Hana's bakery last October. He didn't say, and Hana wasn't there tonight to ask. Oh, I do hope her father isn't worse again. She's always so faithful to attend unless he's sick . . ."

Helina continued to chatter, but Veronika didn't hear another word. *She* was the one who had mentioned their Fellowship meetings when Lady Branden was in Hana's bakery. That meant David's presence tonight was her fault. No! That's not how she should look at it. Christ's love was for everyone. And that included David Branden.

In her bed, Veronika tossed and turned. She sought desperately to soothe her conscience; after all, she had justifiable reasons for her behavior. But God relentlessly searched her soul and pierced her heart with conviction. The truth was that because David's presence disturbed her, she'd exaggerated—no, she'd deliberately lied about her involvement with Boris to avoid spending time alone with David. And now she had both of them to deal with!

Hours later and desperate for peace, Veronika finally resolved that no matter what it cost her in pride, she would have to confess her deception to David and uncover the motive for Boris's possessive behavior.

* * *

David walked toward the boarding house, reflecting on the meeting he'd attended that evening. His heart had soared when they all began to sing. Oh, he'd heard his share of church music, always in Latin, but the worship expressed in everyday language had touched him like never before. He threw back his head and sang the words again.

> *"Fairest Lord Jesus, Ruler of all nature!*
> *Oh Thou of God and man the Son!*
> *Thee will I cherish, Thee will I honor,*
> *Thou my soul's glory, joy, and crown!"*

Their prayers, too, were spoken in their native language, and everyone was given an opportunity to participate. The very idea struck David as intriguing, and it occurred to him that traditional church bored him because the only participation allowed was purely rote. Nothing spontaneous from his heart was ever necessary, much less acceptable. He decided, then and there, that this unusual approach suited him perfectly and he would attend again.

As for the elusive maid, Miss Veronika, maybe there was more to those yellow roses than mere family superstition.

CHAPTER FOUR

Veronika delayed her departure from work on Monday, Tuesday, and Wednesday, determined to talk to David, but each day it grew so late she had to leave before he returned from the university.

Finally, it was Thursday evening. Trepidation filled her heart and slowed her movements while she prepared for Fellowship. If David attended the meeting tonight, she was determined to find an opportunity to confess her deception. And after Boris's startling behavior last week, she may need to deal with him too if he persisted in his territorial behavior. She felt like crying—but what good would that do; it would only make her face red.

When she heard the knocker clatter against the front door, she slid her mother's ring over the knuckle of her third finger, kissed it, and took a bracing breath before opening the door on her evening of anticipated humiliation.

Finding only Helina waiting for her when she stepped out the door, Veronika stared and stammered, "W-Where's Boris?"

"Our Uncle Rudy fell and hurt his back, so Boris left this morning to help the family with their farm chores. He'll be staying until Christmas." Helina grabbed Veronika's arm in a reassuring gesture, "If we stick close together and walk fast on our way home, I'm sure we'll be safe."

Although Veronika nodded and heaved a deep sigh, it wasn't because she'd been worried about their safety; she felt relief that she wouldn't have to decide how to deal with Boris just yet; she knew no matter how tactful she tried to be, he would take it badly.

The two friends walked companionably all the way to the Jamikovi's, and Veronika happily let Helina do the talking.

When they entered the parlor, only three vacant seats remained. Veronika settled in the empty chair beside Eva, but not without noting that David Branden was indeed present. Snatching a covert glance at him, she saw that his blue wool *tabard* matched his bright eyes and a wavy lock of his dark hair fanned across his brow in a boyishly tousled manner. Her mouth went dry. Dear God, how could she ever confess her sin to him? He would surely assume her denial indicated her romantic interest.

Along with everyone else, she bowed her head during the opening prayer, but a desperate plea rose from her troubled conscience: *Forgive me, God, for entertaining such foolishness. I'm afraid I look too much at the outside; I need to remember that You see my heart. Help me to do what's right and only care about what You think of me.*

Sincerely penitent, Veronika kept her thoughts focused during the remainder of the evening. Lucas shared a meditation on humility, which reinforced her resolve to honor God more than man. And when he ended the evening by entreating God's mercy upon their proud souls, she repeated his "Amen."

Following the benediction, Eva reached out motherly arms to Veronika, hugging her warmly before inquiring, "How are Antonin and Jana? I know it's too far for them to walk in this cold weather, but I miss them."

Momentarily distracted from anxious thoughts of her anticipated humiliation, Veronika replied, "Antonin's eyesight is failing, and Jana worries about him a lot. I think she worries about me, too—you know, what will become of me if something should happen to them? But God is good," she made a gamine face, "and I'm young and healthy."

"And pretty, too." Eva smiled, adding with a twinkle, "If you don't mind me saying so." Veronika's eyes brightened at the compliment, but when she returned the smile, she saw that Eva's gaze had shifted to a point beyond her. "Isn't she, David?"

Veronika whipped her head around to find David Branden standing behind her. The warm admiration darkening his eyes sent hers plunging to the floor.

"She is indeed, *Pani* Jamikovi. Very pretty." As David closed the space between them, he whispered, "Boris isn't here tonight, so I'm walking you home."

His closeness and the tangy scent of his soap so disturbed Veronika that she didn't immediately grasp what he'd said. She raised her head and stared wordlessly at him. She hadn't realized he was so tall.

David's mouth twitched in a hint of a grin as he held out her coarse winter garments. "Here's your cloak and hat."

Not wishing to make a scene and knowing she had a confession to make, Veronika didn't argue. When David settled the cloak around her shoulders, she grasped the edges and clutched it tightly to her quaking middle. As hard as she tried to appear relaxed, she couldn't stop the pressure building in her chest because he was standing so close. She felt hot color rush into her face.

Eva smiled indulgently and patted Veronika's arm. "Ah, yes. God is good, very good." Even though Eva said it half to herself, Veronika caught the knowing gleam in her eyes, understood the inference of her remark, and had a sudden desire for the floor to open up and swallow her.

David, out of Veronika's sight, also caught Eva's implication and winked conspiratorially at the older woman.

In the next moment, Helina approached, thanking Eva for making her home available for the group. Instantly, Veronika turned her troubled face to David and spoke in a low voice, "Helina lives just a few houses beyond me. We came together, and she'll need to walk home with us for safety."

David raked his fingers through his dark hair and nodded, but the disappointment clouding his eyes unnerved her. She rushed to say, "I do need to talk to you, though, so maybe we could walk Helina home first."

She knew she sounded forward but it couldn't be helped; she had to talk to him. And it was bad enough

to have to humble herself and confess her dishonesty
to him without Boris's sister listening in.

Helina overheard Veronika's comment and
broke off speaking with Eva to interrupt. "Don't
worry about me. I'll ask Tomas to walk me home."

"You don't need to do that." Desperation gripped
Veronika. She didn't want to spend any more time
than necessary alone with David Branden. Her heart
had become too unruly for her own good.

"Please, come with us. I insist," David quickly
urged, so sincerely that Helina accepted his offer; to
refuse would have been rude.

"You girls lead the way. I'll follow," David
suggested as they emerged into the street.

The early November air was crisp and the clear
evening sky floated over them like a sequined
canopy. The wind whisked along the street, sending
fallen autumn leaves skittering in eddies over the
cobbles and clustering in the doorways. Helina kept
up a monologue that provided a welcome cover for
Veronika's embarrassment.

As they crossed the bridge into Prague's poorer
section, Helina slowed her steps and turned her head
to glance back at David. "Mr. Branden, ever since you

told us how you heard about our meetings, I've wanted to ask you something."

"And what is that?" His deep, rumbling voice sent shivers up and down Veronika's spine.

"Who was the woman your mother overheard talking about our meetings in Hana's bakery?"

Veronika felt her skin prickle. She opened her mouth to confess her role but no sound came out. Wrapping her arms around her middle, she tried to stop the quaking that radiated from the pit of her stomach.

"I don't know; Mother didn't say. You could ask Hana the next time she comes to Fellowship." David paused before adding, "Or you could stop in at her bakery."

Veronika squeezed the words past the constriction in her throat. "There's no need for either. I'm the one she overheard, Helina."

Veronika turned her head and addressed David over her shoulder. "Your mother and sister came into Hana's bakery while I was buying *koláče*. At the time, I didn't know who they were, but I noticed them immediately because your . . . mother is . . . so beautiful." Her words trailed off in an embarrassed whisper.

"Well, Helina, now you know." Amusement tinged David's voice. "Veronika puts us all to shame with her enthusiasm for our meetings."

With her pulse thundering in her ears, Veronika stared straight ahead. Sometimes she didn't know how to take David's comments—had he just paid her a compliment, or was he making fun of her?

As they approached the Marenkova's home, Helina quickly forestalled any drawn-out farewell. "Thanks for walking me home. See you next week. Good night." She quickly darted inside her house and closed the door, leaving David and Veronika alone in the street.

They hadn't gone more than a few steps when Veronika stopped. Her heart felt like it would beat out of her chest, and she could hardly breathe. It was now or never. Grasping her wavering courage with both hands, she cleared her throat and lifted her eyes to David's handsome face, made even more so by the brooding moonlight that emphasized the strong planes of his bone structure and gave his deep-set eyes all the mystery and romance a girl's heart could desire. She caught her trembling lower lip between her teeth and framed her cheeks with her mittened hands.

David stopped. Cocked his head. Waited.

Veronika dropped her hands and faced him squarely. "I-I have a c-confession to make. L-Last week after Fellowship . . ." The lump in her throat would not go down, even when she tried to swallow it.

David didn't interrupt her struggle for words, but it was a good thing his eyes were shadowed or she never would have finished her little speech.

"I deliberately implied that Boris and I," she dropped her gaze and kicked at a cobble with her toe as she groped desperately for the right words, "are more than just friends." There. She'd said it.

"And you're not?" he demanded.

Startled and a bit frightened at his gruff tone, Veronika's eyes darted to his and she shook her head. "N-No, just friends. Since we were ch-children." Her quavering voice betrayed her distress.

His lifted eyebrow told her she hadn't convinced him. Desperate, she protested more vigorously, "Nothing more."

David's eyes narrowed. "Does he understand that's all you are?"

"I-I don't know," she whispered. She hung her head and stared at his chest.

"So you made that implication just to avoid walking with me." It was a conclusion, not a question.

She sighed and swallowed. "I'm sorry I lied." Her confession was a mere thread of sound.

"Hmph. You do wonders for my self-confidence."

Startled by David's statement, she met his reproach-filled eyes. Truly, she hadn't considered his feelings. Hadn't even really thought if he had any. Her mind scrambled wildly for something to say that would repair her inadvertent unkindness. "It's not that I don't like you . . ." she stumbled on, her words drying up under the heat of his glare.

"No?" The word grated between his teeth. "Well, if that's not it, then what is your problem with me?"

Pushed beyond endurance by his disturbing questions coupled with her unruly heart, Veronika exploded, "You've had every advantage life has to offer, yet you always seem so above it all, as if—" her voice shook as her pent-up frustration spilled out in misguided accusation, "as if you expect to be treated as special, and—and even deserve it."

David's lips thinned and his brows rose in shock. Crossing his arms over his chest, he growled, "You're absolutely right. I have had every advantage and probably will continue to." He took a step toward her, demanding, "So why shouldn't I enjoy my life? I see no reason to be miserable unnecessarily. I didn't ask for what I have; it was given to me. So why should you begrudge me?"

"Oh, you—you arrogant waster!"

"How do you know I'm a . . . did you really call me an arrogant waster?" His blue eyes flashed angrily. "I call that unfair. After all, you hardly know me. Why, maybe I'm a gracious benefactor in disguise." He barked a short, mirthless laugh.

"Not likely. I've known other people like you." Brave words, but Veronika knew her protest sounded feeble and unconvincing.

Biting his lip between his teeth, David studied her for a long moment. "Well, I've never known anyone like you." His eerily quiet reply stung her heart more intensely than if he'd spewed biting words. "And if you hadn't given my mother a yellow rose bush, I'd try to forget I ever met you."

Astonishment stole Veronika's voice. She finally managed to resurrect it, scraping out a subdued whisper. "You said something about yellow roses once before. What do they have to do with me?"

"Never mind that now. Come, let's get you home." He grasped her by the elbow and began marching her down the hill.

She stole a look at his ominous face. Further words stuck to the roof of her mouth.

When they stopped at her door, his fingers bit into her arm through the coarse fabric of her cloak as he spun her around to face him. "You are forgiven for misleading me."

His voice was controlled, almost cold, but a ticking muscle in his jaw betrayed his tension. "And just so you don't have to come back later to ask, I forgive you for calling me names."

* * *

David ran all the way to the boarding house, his thoughts pounding in his brain like a smithy's hammer slamming against an anvil. Veronika was right; he might as well admit it. Walking through Lesser Town where she lived had opened his eyes. Truly, he wasn't deliberately unsympathetic. He could see now that he was unexposed and therefore ignorant. Even humble villagers on his father's land lived better than the poor folks here; his father saw to that.

To think that the dainty maid, Veronika, lived among the unfortunate. He'd always imagined that toothless, dirty, crude, and lazy characterized those living in poverty. But the lovely Veronika was anything but unkempt or lacking in intelligence, virtue, or diligence.

His mind wandered back to the gracious hospitality afforded by his ancestral home: the many servants to see to their every need, the open space, the fresh air. Gratefulness welled up in his heart for a second time that evening.

So, why was he so vexed?

He grimaced.

He knew.

He wished he didn't know, but he did.

Veronika had seen through him. She knew he took for granted the ease his privileged life afforded.

He was glad for the darkness; it seemed to hide his shame from the world.

Still, Veronika had seen the truth.

And somehow, her opinion was the only one that mattered.

CHAPTER FIVE

Friday brought a new day, along with an unexpected invitation for David to dine that evening with his mentor's family—and he eagerly accepted the professor's invitation. David knew Veronika's assessment of his character was accurate, but his pride had suffered a stinging blow. Dinner at the Bortskova home was exactly what he needed to boost his spirits. After all, weren't there other girls in the world besides Veronika? Forget family superstition; the professor's granddaughter seemed to like him well enough. Maybe he'd just forget about Veronika and have some fun with Rayna.

Fun! Wouldn't that be a change! No insults. No recriminations. Just admiration and approval. His bruised ego could certainly do with some of that.

Heavy gray clouds had shadowed the sky all day, but David's thoughts were elsewhere. Tonight, he intended to enjoy himself—and the color of the sky was totally irrelevant.

When the two men entered the Bortskova home, the professor excused himself to put away his belongings. David hung his outerwear on one of the hooks above the bench in the foyer, tunneled his long fingers through his dark hair, and drew in a deep breath, relishing the enticing smell of baking bread. It was going to be a good evening; he just knew it.

He heard the soft rustle of Rayna's skirts and her soft-soled shoes scuffing lightly on the stone floor before he saw her.

"I'm so glad you came, David," she welcomed him shyly. "Grandfather said he was going to invite you, but I was afraid you wouldn't come. You're always so busy with your studies and friends."

"I'm glad, too." He looked deeply into her eyes— eyes that were the same warm brown as her grandfather's.

Irena bustled into the doorway, bringing with her the tantalizing aroma of freshly ground cinnamon. "Hello, David. You did come. Good. We'll eat soon." She turned to her daughter. "Come, Rayna. I need your help."

Dinner, like on each previous occasion, proved to be a culinary triumph. Lamb shanks seasoned with salt and rosemary were accompanied by roasted turnips and baby carrots served in freshly-baked crusty trenchers. A steamed apple pudding spiced with cinnamon and garnished with clotted cream finished the meal.

Rayna, all demure smiles, occupied her usual place across from David. For the first time, he really looked at her, noticing her shining brown hair and straight eyebrows. Her teeth were crooked, but her smile was sweet, and her obvious admiration of him infused him with boldness.

Twice he caught her watching him, and he winked at her. And each time, her pale face slowly suffused with a rosy blush as her gaze dropped to her plate. Oh, he was enjoying himself; truly he was, he reassured his conscience's nagging voice.

As dinner concluded, Richard spoke up. "David, I have an urgent business matter to discuss with my father. Would you please excuse us?"

"Of course. That suits me well, too. I need to get back to my studies, this being a week night." The men rose from the table and left the dining room.

When Irena followed them out of the room, saying she needed to speak with a servant, David turned to Rayna. "Would you see me to the door?" He raised his brows over an admiring glance that deliberately intimated more than a courteous leave-taking.

In the hallway, David reached for Rayna's hand, pulling it into the bend of his elbow. Then, instead of walking directly to the front door, he guided her into the parlor and stopped in front of the window.

"Brown is very becoming on you, Rayna," David whispered boldly. He watched her cheeks grow rosy, secretly gratified to know he was the cause.

"Thank you, David." He had to bend down to hear her. "You notice things that nobody else sees."

"Do you think so?" David straightened up, thoroughly pleased with himself. This girl appreciated him. And she had no stuffy conscience to convict him.

Rayna lifted her face to his. Because she was shorter than David, her eyes stopped first at his mouth and then moved up to meet his eyes. Another second, and—well, David wasn't sure what would have happened.

Irena's voice called from the hallway, "Rayna? Has David gone?"

Squeezing Rayna's hand before he released it, David stepped back to a respectable distance as her mother entered the parlor.

"N-No, Mama. We were just talking."

David quickly covered her breathless reply with a smooth diversion, "Thank you for dinner, *Pani* Bortskova. I always feel welcome here."

"You *are* always welcome, David." Irena gave him a satisfied smile and patted his shoulder. "We'll expect you again on Sunday?"

"Yes, indeed. I'm looking forward to it already." He cast a quick glance toward Rayna, who wore her pleasure on her face.

The two ladies walked him to the door and waited, all smiles, while he swung his cloak around his shoulders, tied the cords on his fur hat, and said good-bye.

When the door closed behind him, David found himself standing in pouring rain. Even though he dashed all the way back to the boarding house, by the time he arrived he was thoroughly soaked and chilled to the bone. Shedding his wet things, he draped them over the drying rack near the fireplace and quickly dressed in dry nightclothes. He put more coal on the fire and then climbed into bed, stifling a sneeze.

With his arms crossed under his head, he stared at the ceiling, reflecting on the evening just past. Now that's what he called fun. And his poor, ignored conscience never said a word.

Several hours later, David woke himself coughing. A headache and sore throat added to his misery. He tossed and turned the rest of the night, fluctuating between burning with a fever and shivering with a chill. Breakfast came and went, but David didn't make an appearance.

When Miss Merta carried a pail of coal upstairs to refill his stove, she found his door locked. Immediately, she summoned Miss Hesta.

In response to the housekeeper's vigorous knock, David called in a raspy voice, "Come in."

Miss Hesta inserted the master key into the keyhole, turned it, and opened the door. One glance told her that David obviously suffered from more than the mere discomfort of a cold; his face was flushed and his eyes held a glazed look. But when a severe coughing spasm rattled his whole body, she hurried out to recommend that Widow Flek summon a physician immediately.

Dr. Robosh arrived within the hour. After examining David's eyes, ears, and throat, and putting his ear to David's chest to listen to his lungs, he reported to Widow Flek, "He's a very sick young man and should not be left alone. See to it he drinks a cup of comfrey tea with honey every three hours and keep the steam pan going. I'll come by again tomorrow to check on him. If he's made no improvement, I will bleed him." He went away sober-faced, shaking his head.

Widow Flek ordered Miss Hesta to rotate the servants in staying with David during the day, and she hired an older widow to stay with him at night.

Although boarding At the Stone Swan was costly, even for the smaller rooms, the good widow was known for her charity. And it was whispered among the servants that she was paying for the night care out of her own pocket. Of course, it was in her best interest to be sure no one died while living in her establishment. Nevertheless, it did her reputation no harm to be seen as a benefactress.

* * *

On the fourth day of David's illness, Veronika took her turn attending him. Sitting next to the bed in the room's only chair, she recalled placing the cushion on the seat when she'd first prepared the room. That seemed like such a long time ago. Seeing David so ill now caused her to heap recriminations on herself. He'd taken sick within a day or two after she'd lashed him so cruelly with her judgmental words. That should teach her to mind her tongue.

Jana often said getting sick was related to feeling bad over something. One's heart dictated one's health, to Jana's way of thinking. Dear God, forgive her—David's illness was probably her fault for attacking his character so harshly. And if he died? Well, she'd forever have herself to blame. But how could she live with that guilt?

A knock shook the door and interrupted her heavy thoughts. Veronika rose to her feet as Miss Merta pushed open the door to admit two strangers, a thin, drawn-faced older woman and an equally thin, sloped-shouldered young one.

"*Pani* Bortskova and her daugh'." Miss Merta's eyes apologized for the intrusion. "They're what be perinsistin' to see Mr. David."

Veronika struggled to mask her irritation. Guests were to be directed to Widow Flek, or even Miss Hesta. But Miss Merta obviously didn't remember that. Well, it was too late now; she'd have to manage on her own.

"I'm Miss Veronika," she spoke quietly, approaching the intruders. "How may I help you?"

The young girl blushed and stammered as she gestured toward the bed, "He's—we are . . ."

Mrs. Bortskova immediately lifted her chin and interrupted in a condescending tone that emphasized Veronika's servant status. "Mr. Branden has shown a serious interest in our Rayna, and I expect we'll be announcing the marriage banns by Christmas. It was reported to me that he has taken ill, so I am here to see for myself. "

Veronika's heart skidded to a halt and her breath got trapped in her lungs. Swaying slightly, she crushed one hand in the other as she desperately struggled to regain her balance. David was getting married!

Mrs. Bortskova's eyes narrowed and her voice sharpened, interrupting Veronika's startled thoughts. "I insist that Mr. Branden receive proper medical attention. I suppose he's under the care of a responsible physician." The way she said it implied her doubt.

Veronika's grip tightened until her nails cut into her flesh. The pain centered her mind, and through sheer force of her will she managed to draw in enough breath to speak calmly. "Widow Flek chose Dr. Robosh. He bled David two days ago, and he says we're doing everything that can be done."

"Well, I dare say you're all doing your best," Mrs. Bortskova looked disapprovingly down her pointed nose at the long-handled steam pan used for purging vapors that rested on the small table on the far side of the bed, "but I'll have a word with Dr. Robosh myself. You never can be too careful with fevers." Her gaze shifted to David's inert form, and then before Veronika could discern her intent, she strode haughtily past Veronika toward the bed.

Veronika whirled around in time to see the sharp-tongued woman extend her hand. As her bony fingers stretched out to cover David's hot forehead, her daughter, like a shadow, scuttled after her.

Veronika felt suddenly lightheaded. How little she really knew about David. And those awful things she'd said to him the other night . . . could God ever forgive her?

In the next moment, David moaned. His body twitched involuntarily, causing the down-filled duvet to shift. The bottom end slipped off the bed and pooled on the floor. Mrs. Bortskova paid no attention, but Veronika saw the girl's eager eyes dart to David's bare feet, where black, curling hair grew on his toes.

Protectiveness rose up in Veronika like steam erupting from a boiling kettle; she darted forward and straightened the comforter, pulling it well over David's lower limbs. She felt suddenly hot all over and wished the two ladies would leave her to her own shame.

Clucking her disapproval, Mrs. Bortskova grasped her daughter's slanting shoulder. "Come, Rayna" she commanded. "I must speak with Dr. Robosh." Ignoring Veronika, the two women turned and marched out the door.

Ugh! Veronika thought, closing the door on their retreating figures. The room reeked of their tonics and lotions. She rushed to the window and shoved it open. Would fresh air be good for David? She didn't know, but surely, it couldn't be any worse than the cloying scent left in the wake of those two intrusive women.

Sinking down on the chair beside the bed where David lay fighting for his life, Veronika slumped forward and buried her face in her hands, fighting a battle of her own. That girl had a claim on David; her mother had said it was so. Not that she, Veronika, expected him for herself.

Or did she, in fact, harbor a secret hope? Just thinking about David in a relationship with someone else hurt intolerably.

But then, what did she expect?

She'd avoided him, thinking she wasn't the kind of girl he would choose for his wife. Obviously, this Rayna *was* that kind of girl. And the shock of it served her right for secretly wishing things could be different, for losing her heart to a pair of handsome blue eyes and a charming manner.

"Oh, God." Unaware she'd groaned out loud, Veronika froze when a hot, shaking hand dropped on her head.

Before she had time to think, David wheezed out a hoarse plea, "Please, don't cry. I'll get well. I know I will. Remember the roses?" His hand slid off her hair and dangled lifelessly over the side of the bed, as if the effort had exhausted him.

Veronika gasped and raised her head, her brown eyes brimming with anxiety. David must be delirious. Should she summon help?

But although his voice sounded gravelly, his next words were coherent. "A drink, please."

Veronika vaulted from the chair, her heart pounding at twice its normal pace. She darted around the bed and grasped the handle of the mug resting beside the steam pan on the small side-table. When she came close to offer him the comfrey tea mixed with honey, David opened his eyes, slowly focused on the cup, and then raised his chin slightly.

After a couple of swallows, he sank back weakly and closed his eyes. Groping for her hand, he whispered, "I'm so glad you're here. Promise me you'll stay."

"Yes, I'll stay," she reassured him softly as his fingers twined with hers. *Forever, if you like*, her heart wanted to shout.

* * *

Three days later, Veronika overheard several maids discussing the capable manner in which

Widow Flek had put Mrs. Bortskova in her place. Veronika felt glad that the disapproving woman and her daughter hadn't intimidated her employer. Nevertheless, her own encounter with the two women had left her with a despair she couldn't seem to shake.

CHAPTER SIX

"Why are *you* bringing in the coal, Miss Merta? Where is Miss Veronika?" Before the maid could reply, David's surprise turned into a demand. "Did Miss Hesta rotate your assignments?"

"Oh, no, Mr. David. Miss V'ronika was askin' to trade with me. But I canna 'magine why." Miss Merta smiled at him ingratiatingly before she opened the stove door and added the fresh chunks of coal.

She shook her head. "Miss V'ronika, she's the strangliest girl evah. Oh, not ta be sayin' she is'na nice—she's 'credible nice. Jes' differential, ye know."

"Different?" David turned toward the window to conceal his curiosity.

Miss Merta stared at his back for a moment then chattered freely as she bent to wipe up the coal dust that had spilled. "Oh, she nevah flirts with the uni' boys. An' she's allus goin' ter prayin' meetin's. She's prefectly goodly. Nevah says nuthin bad 'bout nobody, even when someun's mean ta 'er. But she nevah 'as no fun. Least none so's I can tell."

She rushed to add, "Don' be mistakin' me, I'm likin' 'er 'eaps. An' she's the hardinest workin' girl evah. She's the one what trains the new maids, y'know. I s'pose tha's 'cuz Miss Hesta nevah hastah be mindin' 'er 'bout things. Me, I canna be 'memberin' 'strictions from one min' ta the nex'." She laughed loudly, "Course, tha's 'cuz I'm allus thinkin' 'bout what 'tis I'm gonta be doin' when I'm aleaverin' here."

"What do you know about the Fellowship meetings she attends?" David tactfully directed her thoughts. .

Miss Merta sniffed in reaction to the coal dust and shrugged her shoulders. "Nothin'. Miss V'ronka's most er'ligious, but she doesna talk 'bout it muchly. She says 'tis more 'pertant to live that she berlieves. I think she follahs the teachin's of tha' man, Jan Hus, what got hisself burned ta death 'bout fifty years ago. I shouldna say, though, 'cuz I don' be really knowin'. I goes ta Mass 'n Confession reg'lar, an' I save a pinch eachly time I'se gettin' paid ta buy me n'indilgence."

She hastened to explain, "I jes' might be wantin' ta sin real bad suh'time an' then I won' 'ave to be worryin'." She boasted as if she thought herself quite clever to prepare ahead for forgiveness.

David frowned. He'd attended Mass at Burg Mosel every Sunday all his life. But he'd never heard you could buy insurance against your failures. Surely God couldn't be bought off—like He needed the money and sins didn't really matter. This would bear further investigation.

Miss Merta picked up the empty coal bucket. "See ye tomarree, Mr. David," she said glibly, moving toward the door.

"Miss Merta?" She paused and twisted her head around to look at David. "Would you please ask Miss Veronika to come up to see me at some point today?"

Alarm distorted Merta's round face as she hugged the coal bucket. "Oh, Mr. David, you'se not gonta be tellin' 'er what I said 'bout 'er, are ye? I dinna mean nothin' bad fer it, to be sure."

"No, certainly not," he hastened to reassure her. "I just need to discuss a business matter with her."

"Oh. Well, ar'right." Still she hesitated. "If yer fer certain?"

"I'm sure. And thank you for your help today."

* * *

Merta descended the stairs, shaking her head and muttering under her breath, "Mr. David's jes' the mos' richest an' han'somest boarder evah. Why Miss V'ronika tradered 'er chances with 'im, I jes' don' figger."

A few minutes later, Merta discovered Veronika polishing the brass in the parlor. "Mr. David said fer ye to step up ta 'is room when ye were agettin' the chancet. Him's what's gottin some bizziness ta be seein' ye 'bout."

"Oh, Miss Merta," Veronika almost groaned out loud. "Surely you didn't tell him I deliberately traded the care of his room with you?"

"I don't be 'mimberin'," Merta hedged cannily. "We been talkin' 'bout alotsah things, me an' him."

Seeing Veronika's quizzical expression, Merta shot her a sharp glance, "Why don' ye be likin' Mr. David, Miss V'ronka? Him's what's bein' rich—an a real gent'man, too. He nevah shouts ta me when I be aspillin' the coal dust. An' he nevah tries to be pinchin' me or stealin' me kisses."

* * *

Veronika sighed, "Ahh . . . I'd better go see what business he needs to discuss. Excuse me." Veronika dropped her polishing cloth, leaped to her feet, and scurried from the room, determined to escape Miss Merta's bold enumeration of David's virtues.

All the way up the stairs Veronika puzzled over what David could possibly need to discuss with her. He was nearly well now, and he'd never mentioned the day he'd put his hand on her head and assured her he'd get well, even though she'd sat with him several times in the days that followed. She had concluded he didn't remember doing it. But maybe that's what he wanted to talk about.

She smoothed her hair back from her face, straightened her head covering, and shook out her apron before tapping lightly on David's door.

"Who is it?" It had been three weeks since Dr. Robosh assured them David was past the worst, but his lingering cough still roughened his voice.

"Miss Veronika, Mr. Branden. Miss Merta said you wish to see me."

"Yes. Please come in."

Veronika opened the door and stepped inside, leaving it open several inches, like she always did to protect herself. Not that anyone had ever tried to take advantage of her, but it was prudent to be on the safe side. And she instructed each girl she trained to do the same. Not all of them valued their virtue the way she did, but she always emphasized the merit of protecting their employer's reputation and maintaining their dignity.

"What is it you wish to discuss, Mr. Branden?" Veronika hoped her quiet, formal manner would hide her awkwardness. Sometimes, the look in his eyes made her fear he could read her thoughts.

David turned from the window overlooking the rose garden, where a sunken spot served as a constant reminder that she had dug up a yellow rose bush for his mother.

"Please, do sit down," he invited, gesturing toward the cushioned chair. "I won't keep you long, but I have several questions to ask you."

Veronika reluctantly dropped to the edge of the chair that now stood near the stove.

David sank down on the window seat and faced her. His sober expression made Veronika's nerves tingle with anxiety. "I've been thinking a lot about the things you said the night we walked home together from Fellowship."

As remorse billowed over Veronika, she rushed to interrupt—she knew it was rude, but her conscience had upbraided her mercilessly for weeks.

"Mr. Branden, you cannot imagine how sorry I am for what I said to you. It was thoughtless and sinful of me to judge you when I hardly know you."

"Never mind that." Although he waved aside her apology with a dismissive gesture, his eyes narrowed intently. "The point is—you were right. I have been proud and wasteful. Oh, not because I ever meant to hurt anyone. I was just ignorant, I guess. I'm not trying to excuse myself; still, I don't wish to appear any worse than I really am."

A flicker of his old smile tugged at his mouth and warmed his blue eyes before he continued, "I want to beg your pardon for the way I behaved and ask you to be my friend."

"Why, I don't think . . ." She was about to say being his friend was impossible, but she caught herself; realizing the foolhardiness in that made her amend her sentence. "What I mean is, of course you're forgiven, and yes, certainly I'm your friend."

"Will you come up to visit with me occasionally," he requested. "I feel so confined in this room that sometimes I think I'll go crazy. Dr. Robosh says I must wait another week before I go out, because the weather is so frightful just now."

Veronika grimaced; the weather was indeed miserable; it had rained every day for the past two weeks. "Of c-course, Mr. Branden."

"Then, as a friend, may I ask a favor?" At her raised brows he begged wistfully, "Servants, strangers, and children call me Mr. Branden. But as my friend, would you please call me David?"

She wavered for a second before guilt for her judgmental attitude tipped the scale in his favor. "All right. David it is." Anxious to get away, she sprang to her feet. "Is there anything else?"

He looked up, obviously surprised at her rush. "No, not right now," he rose and took a few shaky steps toward her, "but you will stop by again tomorrow to ask how I'm getting along, won't you? I haven't any family here, you know." His boyish expression tugged at her heart.

"But what about . . ." Oh, would she never think before she spoke? It was one of her most glaring faults, at least where he was concerned. Funny, she didn't usually have this problem.

"What about . . . who?" he inquired in a puzzled tone.

"Never mind," she mumbled, but at his commanding expression, she sank back down on the chair, her words following on the tail end of a resigned sigh. "All right, all right." She knew him well enough now to know he would not let her get away with putting him off; once started, he would make her finish.

"While you were sick, a *Pani* Bortskova came to see you. She acted like you were her personal responsibility and made it plain she thought you weren't getting adequate care." She stopped, not mentioning the daughter. She and David certainly weren't close enough friends for her to feel the liberty to ask him for details about his personal life.

He offered nonchalantly, "Oh, her husband's father is my mentor at the university. I've been to dinner at their home a number of times. They knew my father; I suppose that's why they've taken an interest in me."

His inscrutable expression did nothing to prepare her for his next question, the one she'd secretly dreaded. "Did she come by herself?"

Lying wasn't an option; that's what had gotten her into this mess. "N-No, she brought her daughter with her."

"Oh." That was all he said. It told her nothing. Nothing at all.

"So, you will come to see me tomorrow?" he asked again. What a persistent fellow he was.

Her pause was almost imperceptible before she responded to the prompting hope on his face. "Yes, David. I'll come tomorrow." She moved quickly to the door, avoiding his wistful eyes. She wanted no more delays.

His illness-roughened voice followed her, "I'm already looking forward to it."

* * *

Veronika went up to see David every afternoon for the next four days. She sat on the cushioned chair while they talked. About the weather—the rain had finally stopped. About his education—his father had attended Charles University, and David was following in his footsteps. About his religion—the Branden family had been devout for as many generations as David knew about: his parents, his grandparents, his great grandparents.

Veronika told him about her plight as an orphan, and how Antonin and Jana Karska raised her as their own after her mother died. She elaborated that in their younger years the Karska's had been followers of Jan Hus's teachings.

"Many people suffered persecution, even martyrdom, and Antonin said that at one point the Church put a bounty on the heads of Hus's followers: seventy-five gold pieces for a priest, twenty-five for a lay-person. And over five thousand Czech citizens were rounded up and lashed together with ropes and pushed over the edge to their deaths in St. Martin's silver mine at Kuttenberg."

When David gaped at her, she nodded. "And later, the anti-Hussite army surrounded Prague. Jana told me that to intimidate the people in the streets, they shouted over and over as loudly as they could, 'Ha! Ha! Ha! Hus!' Lucas and Eva Jamikovi were one of only a few couples who remained in Prague when Hus's disciples left and established Tabor."

She lowered her voice, "I think the Jamikovi's stayed in Prague because Lucas believes that fighting with those who disagree with you is not pleasing to God. Of course," she sagely observed, "other folk vehemently disagree, insisting that everyone has a responsibility to confront error and correct it, wherever they find it." She furrowed her brow in contemplation. "The two perspectives certainly give one food for thought."

"Anyway," she continued, lifting her chin, "Lucas was one of the city councilmen who helped bring peace back to the city by signing the 'Compactata,' an agreement between the Catholic Church, the moderate Hussite followers, King Zikmund, and the Czech citizens. The treaty guarantees religious options to all, which really means that parishioners like Lucas and Eva are free to hold prayer meetings in their home and priests are permitted to serve the Eucharist to the laity and conduct Mass in German or Czech instead of Latin."

David interjected, "Whoa! I didn't realize such a struggle went into creating the peace we enjoy now. Nobody talks about it here, and I grew up far enough away that I never heard about it. Or maybe I was just too young. But my father attended Charles University in his youth; I'll have to ask him about it when I go home."

"Lucas says we must not forget the lessons of the past," Veronika concluded." He thinks if we take our freedoms for granted, we may lose them due to ignorance or carelessness."

Later that week, in another conversation, David told her a bit about his family. "My great-grandfather, Lord Nicklaus Schmidden, gave a Book of Hours to my great-grandmother, Lady Rose, as a wedding present. It contains Bible verses for each hour of a day, and my grandmother, Lady Rosamund, read them to my sister and me when we were children."

He fleetingly considered mentioning the family fixation with yellow roses, but he hesitated and then decided against it. Veronika wasn't ready for that—and neither was he; he didn't really know what he thought about it. Instead, he described for her the stained glass window depicting a shepherd holding a white lamb that was the focal point in the Chapel of the Shepherd in his ancestral home.

After visiting with David that day, sadness overwhelmed Veronika as she made her way down the stairs. Her knowledge of her birth family and her spiritual heritage was non-existent. Oh, she had her mother's ring. And there was a little old metal box that Jana said had been her mother's. But that was all. Because the box was badly smashed, she'd only succeeded in bruising her fingers the one time she'd tried to pry it open.

And one day when she'd asked about her mother, Jana had replied, "Your pretty mama said that your papa died when a carriage rounded a corner too fast and he couldn't get out of the way because of his having a wooden leg—she said the box was crushed when he was over-run. Your sweet mama died shortly after you were born."

Because it all seemed so sad, Veronika had never asked more questions. After all, she'd told herself, what difference would it make?

The next afternoon when Veronika climbed the stairs to visit David, his door stood open and she could see that he was bundled in his expertly tailored, fur-collared cloak. His matching fur hat dangled by its cords from his fingers.

Veronika's eyes brimmed with questions, but David quickly forestalled her, "Dr. Robosh said I could go out today. But since I'm not to go alone, I asked Miss Hesta if you could accompany me, and she said you may." He quickly added, "That is, if you agree."

His bright eyes full of longing to escape the four walls of his room overcame her reluctance. "Yes, David. I'll go for a walk with you."

While David slowly made his way down the stairs, Veronika slipped into the servants' hall to collect her old brown wool cloak. She was suddenly painfully aware of its shabbiness and the fraying on the ties of her hat. Her worn state was a long-standing condition, but David hadn't seen her winter wear in daylight. As she contemplated telling him she couldn't go, she realized that the root of her problem was pride. Deciding that a substantial dose of humbling would probably do her good, she lifted her chin determinedly and quickly donned her threadbare garments.

Taking no notice of her unfashionable state, David's whole demeanor exuded eagerness when she joined him at the front door.

Looking around the cobbled streets, deserted at that hour of the morning because most folks were at work or school, David filled his lungs with frigid air, stared up at the winter sky, and slowly released a frosty breath before declaring, "You have no idea how good it is to be outside again. For a while there, I thought I might never breathe fresh air again."

As they approached Old Town Square, Veronika waved her hand toward the whitewashed, twin-gabled wood building located across the broad cobble-paved marketplace. "Have you ever attended a Sunday service at Bethlehem Chapel?"

When David shook his head, she continued, "While Jan Hus served as rector of Charles University, he was assigned to the chapel as curate. Every time I go inside, I try to imagine what it must have been like to hear him speak. Lucas said he was a fiery preacher, that he would lean over the pulpit and shout because he was so passionate about the Bible. Did you know he was the one to introduce congregational singing . . . and serving both elements of the Eucharist to everybody, not just the Bread?"

David's head whipped around and he stared at her. "You mean—everyone drinking the Cup, not just the priest?"

"Yes. The Bible says we are *all* to remember our Lord's death."

David frowned and muttered, "I don't know what I think of that idea. It sounds pretty radical to me."

She glanced around and lowered her voice to avoid being overheard. "Lucas and Eva have a Bible. You could stop by their house someday and ask Eva to read that part to you." Her tone brightened, "Or you could come on a Sunday morning and see for yourself."

David leaned toward her, his face suddenly alive with anticipation. "I'd like to come. Do I need a special invitation?"

His eagerness made her laugh, "No, you don't have to be a parish member. Everyone is welcome."

"And what kind of songs do you sing?" The question was simple, but curiosity and admiration mingled on his face.

"Oh, hymns. Worship songs. But not in Latin."

He cast her a thoughtful glance. "I heard *you* sing once. You have a lovely voice."

Her eyes flew to David's face. "You did? When was that?" The question was out before she thought better of it.

He raised his brows and confessed, "The morning you were in my room when I came back from the university to retrieve a lesson exercise I'd forgotten. I heard singing but I didn't know who it was. I tiptoed up the stairs, hoping whoever was in my room wouldn't hear me coming and stop."

She remembered that morning all too vividly and was sure her uneasiness glimmered in her eyes.

"It was a beautiful song. I particularly remember the words because you repeated them several times: *Jezu Ktriste, scedry kneze, Navstev nas a Kriste zaduci.*

"Hearing you sing *Jesus Christ, our generous High Priest, we long for You to visit us,* really moved me," he confided. "I-I made it my prayer."

Veronika felt herself begin to relax, but in the next breath David undid his progress. "But then you traded the care of my room with Miss Merta."

When Veronika kept her eyes straight ahead, he observed laconically, "She does a fine job, of course."

Veronika's heart sank. The very reason she'd initially lied and then traded her duties with Merta was quickly being reinstated in her life in a very different and much more difficult way to resist.

Spending time and thought on David was undoubtedly opening the door to heartache; a young man of his station in life would never marry a penniless orphan like herself. And furthermore, he was soon to be married, so his interest in her must be for an ungentlemanly motive. But there seemed to be no gracious way to avoid him.

When the boarding house came into view, Veronika knew their day's walk was almost at an end.

She wondered how she could feel relieved and sad at the same time.

In the next moment, David turned to Veronika, asking eagerly, "You will walk with me again tomorrow, won't you?"

"I-If you want me to," her words were soft and tentative. She felt so conflicted, so incapable of resisting him.

"I do," David said decisively. "And I'll come to your Bethlehem Chapel next Sunday. I'm sure I'll be well enough to attend by then.

CHAPTER SEVEN

"*Můj bože*, you got to moving early this morning!" Jana exclaimed, sniffing as she saw Veronika stirring the porridge pot.

Veronika glanced over her shoulder. "A friend is planning to visit Bethlehem Chapel for the first time today, so I want to get there early."

Jana immediately questioned, "A friend?"

In response to Jana's quizzical expression, Veronika swung around to face Jana. Her tone held a trace of annoyance. "Yes, Jana, my friend is a young man. He's a student at the university and one of our boarders. He's the one I told you about who's been so sick. He's better now, but while he was recovering we talked a lot about what we believe. He's curious about our hymn-singing—and everyone participating in the Eucharist."

Jana immediately picked up on Veronika's defensiveness. "Don't you be getting ideas about marrying him, Roni. That's trouble you'd be asking for, setting your affection on one who doesn't share your freedom of faith. We love you too much to see you make that choice."

"I doubt he would entertain such a thought. He's the son of a lord and his family owns a huge estate." Veronika shrugged. "I'm not the sort of girl he'd choose for a wife. Besides, I think he's already committed to someone else."

Despite her disclaimer, Veronika's voice and eyes betrayed her heart, and Jana perceived that damage had already been done. This young man may not consider their girl suitable to be his wife, but Veronika was in love with him—there was no doubt. She, Jana Karska, may be old, but she hadn't forgotten the look of love.

Oh, God, why had this happened?

Well, she'd just have to pray harder, that's all.

* * *

Daylight hours were safe for walking alone, and Veronika did want to arrive early, in time to visit with friends and, yes—to greet David, she admitted with a twinge of guilt over her happy anticipation. But standing water resulting from a heavy rain during the night covered the street in places.

Veronika stepped carefully in her *pattens,* elevated wood soles strapped to her shoes, to avoid the worst of the water, but by the time she reached the Stone Bridge, she was certain she'd be late.

Clattering across the long, hundred-year-old sandstone bridge, she concentrated so intently on avoiding puddles that she forgot to laugh as she usually did about the good village women from all over Czech who'd sent cart-loads of raw eggs to be used in the mortar, so the bridge would be solid— and the women of Velvary, who'd hard-boiled theirs so they wouldn't break during the cart-ride, thus rendering them useless.

Approaching Old Town Square, Veronika immediately looked up toward the Prague Orloj, the astronomical clock in the tower that loomed over the marketplace. Encircled by golden numerals on a black ring, the dials on the unique timepiece indicated the positions of the sun and moon. A quick glance told her that she still had fifteen minutes before the bell rang out the hour. Inhaling deeply of the rain-washed air, she hurried on.

When the bell tolled just as she approached Bethlehem Chapel, she knew there would be no time for visiting, but she was glad to be on time. She paused outside the door to catch her breath before she entered the open, vaulted-ceiling hall that could easily accommodate three thousand people.

The plastered walls featured a few paintings with hymn lyrics scripted below them, but there was a noticeable lack of side chapels, icons, statues, confessionals, or other elements of religious ritual; the room's purpose as a preaching hall was evident in its general plainness, in keeping with Jan Hus's teachings on pure religion and simple lifestyle that he'd gleaned from the writings of the martyred Englishman, John Wycliffe.

Veronika scanned the rows of chairs and stools that filled the room. She saw Hana, holding Dasha on her lap, seated about halfway toward the front on the center aisle. The row ahead of her held Eva and Lucas seated side-by-side with his arm resting around her shoulders. Tomas sat next to Lucas. And was that David Branden's dark head beside Tomas's white-haired one? Her heart skipped a beat. So, he had come.

David turned then and spotted her. With a smile and a nod, he stood and waved his hand, beckoning her to join him.

Veronika felt her cheeks grow hot. Now her friends would associate them together. Well, she certainly did seem to have more than her share of pride. God forgive her, she'd better swallow it and think more about others and less about herself. David considered her his friend—and that's what she would be.

When Veronika slipped into the empty seat beside David, he caught her glance and leaned toward her, whispering in a friendly tone, "Did the rain delay you?"

She nodded as she sank into her chair. "I went around as many puddles as I could, so I was afraid I'd be late. And my *pattens*," she glanced at her feet with a wry expression, "slowed me down even more because I tried not to splash."

As the town clock finished signaling the hour, everyone immediately quieted. Then heavy, rapid footsteps clacked on the stone floor, awkwardly interrupting the hush. Veronika looked up as Boris and Helina made their way down the side aisle and stopped at the end of the row in front of them where there were several empty chairs.

Veronika felt her heart drop to her stomach; Boris was back!

Following Helina between the chairs, Boris's gaze fixed intently on Veronika. In the next instant, his eyes narrowed on David, seated beside her, and then shifted back to Veronika. His brows rose, framing a piercing glare, before he slouched into his seat with a low growl.

Squeezing her hands together in her lap and fixing her eyes on the choristers as they filed in through the side door, Veronika determined that nothing, not even the ill-tempered Boris, would draw her attention away from participating in worship.

When the singers were assembled, she turned her attention to the elevated preaching pulpit with its sound-amplifying canopy, the focal point of the meeting hall, and felt dismay to realize that Boris's shaggy head blocked her view. In the next moment the choir rose and began to sing. Closing her eyes, Veronika concentrated on the words of their opening song, *Hospodine, Pomiluj Ny!*

As the final "Lord, have mercy!" faded away, a rotund, balding man climbed the enclosed wooden steps and entered the pulpit. When David glanced at Veronika with a question in his eyes, she shifted toward him so she could see around Boris' head and then quietly identified the man as Brother Henrik, the present curate.

After the choir sat down, Brother Henrik read in his sonorous voice from the fifth chapter of Matthew's gospel: "*Blessed are the pure in heart: for they shall see God.*"

His simple homily challenged the congregants to examine their motives, search their hearts, repent for harbored sin, and make every effort to please God with a pure heart.

Veronika pressed her lips together; she knew she struggled with pride. Concern about what others thought of her often affected her attitude toward them, toward herself, and ultimately toward God.

A simple and sincere prayer rose from her heart: *Dear Father, help me value Your approval above all. And forgive me for my foolish heart that wants what it cannot have.*

* * *

David, hearing the truth spoken in the common language, felt genuine conviction for the first time in his life. And when Brother Henrik asked the congregants to examine their hearts before coming

119

forward to receive the elements of the Eucharist, David bowed his head.

But Brother Henrik didn't stop there. He quietly suggested that if anyone's heart had been touched by the Scripture verse or the homily, all one needed to do was acknowledge and repent for one's sin. Forgiveness would be granted.

In childlike simplicity, David closed his eyes and silently confessed his faults and failures and asked God for forgiveness. The cleansing sensation that followed his simple, sincere prayer shocked him. He straightened his shoulders, quite as if a load had lifted off him; he felt refreshed and lighthearted. He had dutifully made regular confession for his childhood pranks to Father Andrew and his successor, Father Klemens, but he'd never before connected *with God* to repent and receive absolution for his selfish motives and ungrateful attitude.

When Brother Henrik spread his hands above the chalice and charger for the Blessing of the Bread and the Cup, David noted in surprise that they were simple wooden vessels, not ornate, bejeweled gold objects like those in the chapel at home.

"Come, Holy One, come. Bless and prosper this meal; bless and prosper this fellowship; bless and prosper our lives, that justice and love may be the measure of our common witness."

Following the "Amen," the chairs emptied out as row after row of worshipers went forward to kneel. Brother Henrik moved along the line, placing a flat wafer on each parishioner's tongue. The chalice followed, handed along for each one to take a sip and pass to the next person.

When Tomas stood to lead their row to the front, David vaulted to his feet and eagerly followed. For the first time in his life he felt a rush of anticipation for a public demonstration of his faith.

As Veronika knelt beside him at the altar, David glanced over at her bowed head. His heart leaped with joy; this was something they could share, something spiritually significant they now had in common. He closed his eyes, focusing on the meaning of the elements, sensing that his participation today marked a rite of passage in his spiritual journey.

After everyone had been served and had returned to their seats, the entire congregation began to sing a doxology:

"Glory be to the Father, and to the Son, and to the Holy Ghost. As it was in the beginning, both now and always . . ."

David had never experienced anything like it; God Himself seemed to fill the room. He wondered if his heart would burst from joy. To think he'd been missing this all his life. His parents were devout believers, faithful and dedicated, pious and upright, but oh, surely they had not experienced the joy he now felt. Either that or he'd been unbelievably insensitive for years. Serving God had seemed a dull and uninteresting business; necessary, of course, but a burdensome duty. But not so, what he'd experienced today. He wanted to shout with delight from the bottom of his soul.

When the final notes died away, Brother Henrik invited everyone to repeat the Apostle's Creed. David knew it by heart in Latin, having religiously intoned it week after week for as long as he could remember. But today, spoken in everyday language, the significance of the words gripped his heart.

I believe in God, the Father Almighty, Creator of heaven and earth; and in Jesus Christ, His only Son, our Lord: Who was conceived by the

Holy Spirit, born of the Virgin Mary; suffered under Pontius Pilate, was crucified, died, and was buried. He descended into hell; the third day He rose again from the dead; He ascended into heaven, is seated at the right hand of God the Father Almighty; from thence He shall come to judge the living and the dead . . .

Following the final benediction, the congregants surged to their feet, greeting each other with enthusiastic hugs. Veronika quickly moved into the aisle to greet the worshipers who spilled into the aisle nearest her. David glanced around, startled by the overt display of affection taking place around him.

When he slowly rose to his feet, Eva immediately reached out to him with a motherly hug and planted a kiss on his cheek. As she released him, there was someone else to take her place. He got soundly embraced many more times before it was all over.

Straightening from the last hug, David's attention was snagged by little Dasha, who was squeezing between grown-up legs as she pushed through the crowd calling "*Teta* Roni!" in her shrill child's voice.

Upon reaching Veronika, the child threw her arms around Veronika's legs, eliciting parishioners' affectionate smiles.

Bemused, David watched Veronika bend down to return the little girl's hug. With his next breath the activity around David faded; he saw only the pretty maid stooped tenderly over the small child's eager, uplifted face.

In that moment, an inexplicable longing for what his future could hold swept over David. A family. A wife. A child of his own. A child to sing to and rock, to bounce on his knee, to hug and to cuddle. A child who would be a result of love, who would respond to and return that love.

While David watched in a trance-like state, Dasha giggled and pulled free. Skipping happily, the little girl rushed away to find her mother.

As the vision faded, David wiped his hand over his face and found himself putting one foot in front of the other, his gaze fixed on Veronika as he moved toward her. And in a sudden moment of clarity, he knew he wanted that future; he wanted her.

CHAPTER EIGHT

On Monday afternoon, Veronika joined David for their daily walk. "Everyone seems in such a hurry," she commented as students and business people, wrapped warmly against the cold, scurried past them with barely a glance. They passed the university and then ambled along the riverfront.

David seemed pensive, but Veronika resisted questioning him; she didn't want him to think she was nosy. And he didn't tell her what was troubling him until they neared At The Stone Swan at the conclusion of their walk.

"This is our last afternoon together. Dr. Robosh has given me permission to resume my studies and to return to school."

"Oh," Veronika's gentle smile hid her sadness, "but that means you are well again!"

"Yes, I suppose it does—" David's tone grew more cheerful, "and I'm certainly glad to be well." He turned his attention to her upturned face. "But I'll miss our walks. Maybe I can think up some other way to spend time with you." His blue eyes twinkled, "I *am* pretty creative, you know."

They both laughed. For the first time since his illness, David sounded like his normal, jaunty self.

* * *

On Tuesday, Professor Bortskova reminded David of the still-standing regular Sunday evening dinner invitation at his home.

David hesitated. What should he do? He deeply regretted flirting with Rayna the last time he'd been to the Bortskova home for dinner, and subsequent embarrassment left him feeling awkward.

"Well, will you come?" his professor pressed him.

He had to make a decision; to delay any longer would appear rude and ungrateful. "Same time?" he managed.

"As usual," Professor Bortskova affirmed.

"All right. I'll be there." David's hesitancy and lack of enthusiasm made his mentor study him speculatively as he hurried out of the classroom.

The Sunday night dinner quickly slipped from David's mind as his thoughts surged forward to Thursday evening when he would again see Veronika.

Over the next two days his mind wandered from

his studies more times than he cared to admit. And when a fellow-student caught him staring into space and questioned him about his obvious preoccupation, David wiped his hand over his face, mumbling, "Just not up to my old self yet."

The lad shot a skeptical glance at David's flushed face before he jumped on his lame excuse, proclaiming loudly in a lyrical chant, "David's sweet on a gi-rl; David's sweet on a gi-rl." Several other classmates joined in teasing him, but David just shrugged his shoulders and ignored them.

The days dragged on in slow motion, and by Thursday, every minute seemed an hour. When dinner was served in the boarding house, David's impatience to see Veronika had so overtaken him that he wolfed down his meal and rushed off with hardly a civil greeting to the other boarders.

Eva answered David's knock on the Jamikovi's door, and when she saw who it was, she greeted him warmly. "David, come in, come in."

As soon as he stepped inside she reached for his cloak, suggesting, "Why don't you wait in the parlor for the others to arrive. The Bible is open on the lectern. Feel free to read a bit."

David cleared his throat and tried in vain to suppress his eagerness. "Will you show me the part about everyone participating in Holy Communion?"

Eva led the way into the parlor and approached the large book that lay open on the wooden lectern standing in the corner. She carefully turned the pages to First Corinthians, chapter eleven. "Start here," she said, marking a spot with her index finger.

When David had put his finger where hers had been, she turned to leave. "I'll be back shortly."

"All right," David mumbled distractedly; he could hardly wait to read the verses for himself.

". . . the Lord Jesus on the same night in which He was betrayed took bread; and when He had given thanks, He broke it and said, 'Take, eat; this is My body which is broken for you; this do in remembrance of Me.'
In the same manner He also took the cup after supper, saying, 'This cup is the new covenant in My blood. This do, as often as you drink it, in remembrance of Me. For as often as you eat this bread and drink this cup, you proclaim the Lord's death until He comes.'"

As David read through the passage a second time, and then a third, his heart responded to the living words. Yes, the bread *and* the cup are for me. And for everyone who believes!

Why had he never heard this before? No one at home seemed to know anything about it. Oh, there was the Book of Hours in the Chapel of the Shepherd and Father Klemens read from his copy of the Bible on Sundays and holy days, and he'd learned Latin by studying specifically assigned passages, but his soul had never been moved with a yearning to read the scriptures.

Then and there, a resolve entered David's soul: He would buy a Bible—his own Bible. Surely one could be had if money weren't an issue. He would look into it immediately. For all he knew, the Bible might contain other things he'd never heard before.

"How are your studies coming, David?" Eva inquired as she re-entered the parlor. "I've been praying that you'd be able to catch up on everything you missed."

Lost in thought, David was slow to turn to her. But when her words registered, he was quick to reply. "Truly, God has helped me. I've spent every evening since my recovery reading or debating with other students, and I'm happy to say I've caught up in every discipline."

"Good. Very good." She paused. "And how is Miss Veronika?"

A shadow fell over David's face and he looked away. After a heaving breath, he said slowly, "I really don't know; I haven't seen her since Monday. She's gone by the time I get back to the boarding house." Then as if he just had to tell someone, he met her gaze and confided in a hopeful tone, "I could hardly wait for tonight."

Eva's smile held sympathetic understanding.

"I'm planning to invite her to attend Mass with me at St. Vitus's Cathedral next Sunday morning. She said once that she would love to go there sometime, so I stopped in yesterday to inquire after the service schedule."

Eva spontaneously offered, "Why don't you two come here for a meal afterwards. We'd love to have you join us." Her enthusiasm was contagious.

David's countenance brightened. "I'd like that." He added, "I'll check with Veronika and let you know if we can come."

When the knocker clattered, interrupting their conversation, Eva excused herself to greet the folks waiting outside her door. David claimed a straight-backed chair but he was far too excited to make himself sit down; he paced back and forth, restlessly anticipating Veronika's arrival. But after a few minutes, impatience got the better of him, and he headed toward the entry hall.

As David rounded the corner, Tomas broke off visiting with Eva to greet him with a hearty welcome. "Hello, my friend. Glad to see you."

"And you." David returned the greeting. But when the knocker clattered again, his eyes strayed toward the door.

Boris and Helina entered the hall, but David's heart sank when he realized that Veronika was not with them. He turned away, concluding she must not be coming.

In the next moment, he heard a child's treble voice announcing, "Here we are, Teta Roni!" David swung around in time to see Dasha bound eagerly through the doorway, dragging a laughing Veronika after her into the spacious entry hall.

David's heart jumped in his chest. With her head thrown back and her cheeks rosy from the cold, he thought she'd never been more beautiful. He stood off to the side, waiting while Veronika assisted Dasha in removing her heavy winter wear and then removed her own. Eva welcomed each of them with a warm hug and collected their wraps.

When Veronika, who was last in line, handed Eva her cloak, David moved close and whispered her name, "Veronika." He couldn't completely stifle the hunger in his voice.

"David," she exclaimed softly, turning toward him and lifting her eyes to meet his. Watching her lips shape his name made his pulse thrum erratically.

He reached eagerly for her hands, pressing them in his own. "I've missed you."

Under his steady gaze her cheeks flushed pink. She tugged at her hands in an effort to release them from his disturbing touch.

But he refused to let go.

"Aren't you glad to see me?" he questioned impetuously. As his eyes searched hers, the door opened, admitting Hana and Milan on a blast of frigid air.

Veronika instantly stopped tugging. "Shh! Of course I am," she murmured. But even as she said the right words her face told a different story.

Hurt scratched David's heart, but he marked her reticence to maidenly modesty. Dropping her hands, he angled himself so he could speak to her without being overheard. "I went by St. Vitus's Cathedral yesterday. There is a Mass at nine o'clock each Sunday morning. Would you care to go with me this coming Sunday? And afterwards, Eva has invited us to join them here for the mid-day meal."

Caught completely off guard, Veronika blinked several times. She swallowed hard, color coming and going in her cheeks. Why was he inviting her to spend time with him when he was promised to someone else?

Sensing her indecision, David appealed, "Please, come as my friend."

"All right," she finally agreed. But her reluctance dampened his pleasure. Winning Veronika's heart was requiring every form of skill and tact he'd ever learned. And some he had yet to acquire.

* * *

Veronika spent another sleepless night tossing and turning in her narrow bed. This road leading to heartache could have been so joyous. When David had extended the invitation to attend Mass with him on Sunday at St. Vitus's Cathedral, her heart had shot into her throat. For a moment, she'd felt dizzy with delight.

And then she'd remembered.

Rayna.

Everything she wanted to share with David was happening—except that it wouldn't be hers to keep; she wasn't the kind of girl David would choose to marry. And when David married Rayna, she'd be left with empty memories and a broken heart.

Veronika's pillow caught a few tears before she realized that rejecting David's friendship stemmed only from thinking about her own selfish desires. Over the years, she'd watched Antonin and Jana lovingly interact and had innocently anticipated someday experiencing the sweet intimacy they shared as husband and wife.

In truth, she'd had no idea love could hurt so much. But if she truly did love David, then she needed to release her expectations. God loved her unconditionally. If she wanted to be like Him, she would have to love His way. Generously. Freely. Unselfishly.

With righteous resolve, she determined to put her heart on ice and continue as David's friend. But the anticipation and agony she experienced just contemplating spending Sunday with him left her on edge and without appetite. And to make matters worse, Jana chided her at meal times when she pushed her food around and scarcely managed to choke down a few bites.

Joyce Brandt Williams

CHAPTER NINE

Nauseated. That's how Veronika felt when she woke on Sunday morning. Desperate longing to see David had gnawed at her heart all week, yet she knew that every minute spent with him today would be a most exquisite torture.

She donned her blue Sunday *cotte*—the dress certainly wasn't new, but at least there were no patches on the elbows—and quickly slipped into her pointed-toed shoes to shield her feet from the cold floor. From a center part she rolled her hair up and back over her ears and then worked it all into a braid. Not for the world would she let David know she was bleeding emotionally. She slipped her mother's ring over her third-finger knuckle, kissed it, and collected her cloak, mittens, and hat.

Skipping breakfast—she couldn't stomach a single bite—she was ready well before the appointed time. Moving to the window, she waited. When she saw David walking up the street and heard his soft whistle, she slipped outside to meet him; Antonin and

Jana were still sleeping and she didn't want him to rap the knocker and wake them.

David fell into step beside her without saying a word, but he kept stealing sideway glances at her. Finally, her curiosity got the better of her.

"Is something wrong with me? Do I have something on my face?" she burst out diffidently, swiping her hand across her mouth. "Why do you keep staring at me?"

David, usually so eloquent, stammered, "What? Oh. No, nothing's wrong—at least, not with you!" He hesitated, and then burst out boyishly, "It's just that you're so beautiful. And I'm asking myself how I came by the good fortune to spend the day with you."

"You asked," she replied so unaffectedly that he laughed.

"I know that," he flashed his charming smile, "but it seems God had something to do with directing our paths. You've brought so many wonderful things into my life, how can I ever thank you?"

If only the look in his eyes meant what she longed for it to mean. Oh, the pain that accompanied secret love. "Don't give it another thought," she answered through a throat that felt stuffed with cobwebs. "That's what friends are for." She was determined to do and say the right things, even if her heart bled to death.

They climbed the hill to the Hradcany royal grounds, watching the cathedral's spires and turrets rise up before them as they approached the Golden Portal, the church's main entrance. Above the Portal, the eighty-two square meter mosaic composed of jewel-toned Bohemian glass depicted the Last Judgment: Jesus surrounded by angels and kneeling Czech patrons: Saints Prokop, Zikmund, and Vitus on the left and Saints Wenceslas, Ludmila, and Vojtech on the right. Veronika shuddered at the menacing gargoyle-faced drains perched along the roofline, especially when David reminded her that they were believed by some to scare away evil spirits.

Moving toward the entrance, they found it easy to mingle with the crowd already streaming into the imposing edifice. Once inside, Veronika tipped her head and looked up. Her eyes grew wide; she'd never seen anything so magnificent in her life. The ribbed ceiling arches seemed to reach into heaven. How did they manage to stay up there? And high above the altar, the stained glass rose window burned with brilliant ruby color. Long ribbons of rosy morning sunshine caressed the furnishings, icons, and paintings. The High Altar, a masterpiece in gold and embellished with sparkling jewels, would have been gaudy in any other setting, but here, it seemed appropriate.

After they found seats close to the front, Veronika studied the architecture, the paintings, and the adornments. Most fascinating were the auxiliary chapels containing chest-high marble tables or carved stone sarcophagi, where parishioners clustered, performing pre-service rituals.

A sad-faced young woman carrying a votive entered the little side chapel closest to their seats. Through the smoky haze, Veronika watched her touch the small candle's wick to a burning candle. When the flame leaped up, she placed it among the hundreds of already-burning vigil lights in varied heights and sizes that rested on the table, the floor in front of the table, and the candle stands behind it.

The woman genuflected and then backed away to sit on the stone bench facing the table. While silent tears streamed down her pallid cheeks, she bowed her head and fingered her prayer beads, her lips moving in silent prayer.

Veronika's face reflected her pity for the girl's heartache, and David, noting her compassionate expression, whispered an explanation. "The candle flame is meant to carry her prayers to heaven. As long as the candle is burning, her prayers are going up."

Their conversation was sidetracked by the hush that fell over the congregants when a priest, clothed in a black robe topped with a belted white surplice, moved down the central aisle. He carried a gold *ciborium*, a lidded cup containing the Blessed Sacrament. An *acolyte*, the priest's assistant, followed him, swinging an incense-puffing censor. As the Latin liturgy began, familiarity made David a skilled participant, and he tactfully assisted Veronika whenever she hesitated.

From the beginning of the service, Veronika felt like she'd been exiled to a foreign country. The Mass was conducted in Latin, the priest served himself the Eucharist, and the chants were sung in Latin. It was all beautiful—in an ethereal sort of way, but now she understood why Jan Hus passionately preached and facilitated interactive connection with God.

When the service concluded, David helped Veronika to her feet and placed a hand on her shoulder to guide her toward the door. There was a heavy press of people, as if now that they had done their duty, they wanted to get on with their lives— not at all like the worshipers' warm affection for each other and their reluctance to leave Bethlehem Chapel, Veronika thought.

They made their way in silence through the crowd and then down the hill from the royal grounds, both lost in private thoughts. As they began walking along the street, David turned to Veronika. His blue eyes beneath dark brows brimmed with curiosity. "Well, what did you think?"

Veronika's mouth went suddenly dry. She answered slowly, not wishing to offend him, yet endeavoring to be honest. "It was all very beautiful— in a mystical sort of way. But I felt so sad for the young woman crying in the little side chapel; she seemed so hopeless." She stopped for a bracing breath before blurting, "Why should folks who are able to purchase the tallest, most expensive candles get the most attention from God?" She dropped her eyes, half afraid of his reply.

After a few moments of startled consideration, David confessed, "I never thought of it that way, but the truth is, I've never given any thought to the rituals." He made a wry face and rolled his eyes in chagrin. "I'm afraid I wasn't a very apt pupil. My mother seldom complained, but I know my lack of interest in religious matters disappointed her."

Veronika remained silent, her eyes again fixed on his face.

Slowly, David's countenance brightened, as if in his reflecting he was experiencing a revelation. "My father was more understanding; he always said spirituality was a matter of the heart. Now I know he was right, but at the time I had no idea what he meant. And no one ever explained it to me. I've heard those same words all my life, but today, for the first time, I really understood them! Thank you!"

Carried away in his enthusiasm, David whooped a glad cry and caught Veronika in a bear hug. Sweeping her off her feet, he swung her around.

Veronika forgot all about the inequity of candles and prayers as they related to God's justice. Held in David's strong arms and pressed close to his heart, her self-control suffered a violent assault that shook her all the way down to her small toes in her pointed shoes.

Giddy as a schoolboy and oblivious to Veronika's stunned reaction, David dropped her back down on her feet, tossed his hat in the air, and whirled around.

Statue-still, Veronika watched him through burning eyes. She hardly breathed for fear she would explode; her emotions roiled like a boiling kettle over a blazing fire.

Friendship with David? That she could handle.

Being clasped in his embrace with his face so near to hers that she could see the faint shadow of his beard on his upper lip, jaw, and chin? *Bože můj!* That was almost more than she could bear.

David swooped, caught up his hat, and smashed it down over his dark hair. Then facing her, he marched, skipped, danced backwards, talking non-stop all the way to the Jamikovi's home. His own enthusiasm blinded him to the fact that Veronika did not utter a single word.

Lucas greeted them heartily at the door, and Eva joined him, welcoming them inside with warm hugs. When they were seated around the food-laden table in the Jamikovi's large dining room, Lucas offered a simple grace.

As they began to eat, David enthusiastically described their visit to the cathedral, mentioning Veronika's previously stated impressions and his own thrill of excitement at discovering spiritual life in the words of the liturgy.

Veronika picked at the nut-crusted meatballs served with spicy red-pepper salad in crusty trenchers. She said very little. A nerve twitched in her left eye, and she felt cold all over. Struggling to remain attentive, she took a deep swallow of the honey-sweetened mead creamed with an egg and spiced with cinnamon and cloves, hoping the hot drink would warm the cold despair that seemed to permeate every cell in her body.

Although Eva tried to engage Veronika in conversation, her guest barely managed yes and no answers to each question. Sensing Veronika's struggle over something she chose not to share, Eva tactfully directed their attention to the conversation between Lucas and David.

When everyone had finished eating, the foursome lingered around the table as the men chatted for another hour.

Finally, during a brief lull in the conversation, David glanced over at Veronika. When her wan smile failed to warm her face or reach her eyes, he abruptly pushed back his chair and leaped to his feet.

"I have been shockingly thoughtless; we've stayed far too long. Veronika works hard all week, and this should be a day of rest for her."

Within minutes, Eva had retrieved their cloaks. When they were bundled against the cold, they expressed their thanks and exchanged good-byes.

Once David and Veronika were out on the street, silence hung awkwardly between them as they headed for the Karska's home. Veronika knew David kept glancing at her in an effort to make eye contact, but she couldn't risk letting him see the truth she was sure would shine from her eyes—that she loved him, loved his keen mind, loved his enthusiasm. Instead, she opened her eyes wide to disguise the unbidden tears that prickled behind them.

When David finally spoke, remorse weighted his words, "Will you please forgive me for being so thoughtless and inconsiderate?"

His entreaty was nearly her undoing, but Veronika forced her lips into a semblance of a smile as she whispered gently, "There's nothing to forgive, David." After all, she knew David wasn't the problem.

She lifted her eyes to meet his worried ones. "I think that visiting such a big place overwhelmed simple little me. But I do thank you. Attending Mass at the cathedral was something I've always longed to do, and you made that possible. Please don't think I didn't have a good time—I did. It was wonderful . . . maybe just a little too wonderful."

She quickly covered her errant sob with what she hoped would pass for a chuckle, and was relieved when David showed no indication of having perceived her distress.

"Thank you for going with me," he said as they approached her door.

"Good-bye, David," she managed in an overly bright voice before she hurried inside, hoping he wouldn't see the gush of tears she could no longer hold back.

***

David returned to At The Stone Swan, completely at a loss to understand Veronika. What had he said or done to put that strained look on her face? Surely, the day hadn't been that tiring.

He quickly freshened up and set out for the Bortskova's, arriving on time for dinner. However, his thoughts frequently strayed, and he ate very little even though it was his favorite roasted chicken with lemon custard for an after-sweet.

As they neared the end of the meal, Irena confronted him forthrightly. "David, what is troubling you? You've hardly eaten a bite of your dinner and you've only said six words since you arrived. You're not feeling unwell again, are you?"

"What?" David exclaimed, startled out of his thoughts. "Oh, no, I'm quite well." He frowned, then struggled to explain, "I-I'm trying to figure out a difficult problem, that's all."

"Well, maybe if you told us about it, we could help you solve it," Richard suggested, producing the longest sentence David had ever heard him speak. "It wouldn't have something to do with a certain young woman, now would it?" He waggled his brows knowingly.

David felt his face grow hot. He quickly lowered his gaze and stared at his plate.

Irena winked reassuringly at Rayna before she gave David's arm an encouraging pat and offered him a motherly lifeline, "Don't worry, my boy. It will all work out. Especially if you're both fond of each other."

David stared at his plate and nodded, so lost in his misery that he didn't catch her wink or perceive her meaning. "I'm sure you're right," he muttered in a valiant effort to be agreeable. "Everything will work out eventually."

Joyce Brandt Williams

CHAPTER TEN

It was Thursday. David hadn't seen Veronika since their Sunday visit to St. Vitus's Cathedral and the subsequent lunch at the Jamikovi's. After tomorrow, the university would be closed for Christmas break. David completed a rhetoric examination in the afternoon and then headed straight to the Jamikovi's home, arriving just as Eva returned from an outing to the fabric guild.

"Come in, David," she invited. "What a pleasant surprise!"

As he stepped inside, Eva instructed her maid, "Take David's cloak and bring us each a mug of hot spiced cider and some of the fresh *koláče* that cook baked this morning."

David followed her into the parlor, where she deposited her purchases on a bench and immediately launched into describing her plan to surprise Veronika by sewing her a new *cotte* for Christmas. She had the cobalt blue silk fabric spread out over a chair before she interrupted herself, apologizing with a chuckle, "Oh, do forgive me, David! I'm just a garrulous old woman who loves a certain pretty girl and can't help getting excited over bringing a little happiness into her life. Now, I know you didn't come by to hear me prattle on about fabric and patterns, so come, let's have a little refreshment, and we'll enjoy a good visit."

As the maid entered the room, Eva gestured for David to be seated on the padded settee and then seated herself on a nearby tall-backed chair.

The maid deposited a polished wood serving tray on a side table. At a nod from Eva, she proceeded to serve them each a jam-filled pastry and a handled pewter mug topped with a lid.

Eva dismissed the maid with a nod and then repressed a smile as she watched David press on the thumb lever and raise the lid, inhaling the spicy steam with a sigh of pleasure.

They sipped their cider and munched on the sweet refreshments for a few minutes before Eva turned to David. "So," she invited conversation. "tell me why you've come to see me."

David swallowed his last bite of pastry, cleared his throat, and then gulped another swallow of cider.

Feeling awkward about discussing a personal matter with a woman—especially one who was not his mother, David opened his mouth to tell her he'd come to read again in the Bible. But the kindness in Eva's eyes disarmed his reticence, and the truth spilled out: He simply did not understand Veronika. Could Eva give him some insight?

Eva's face conveyed compassion and affection. The world was full of young men, but this one was exceptional; he had a dignity of bearing and an innate charm that distinguished him, even in a crowd.

"David, I don't have an answer, or any advice, either," she said kindly. "But I do know Someone who has both. Let's ask Him to help you."

He nodded, his eyes haunted by despair. "Yes, please," he whispered, returning his mug to the tray. "I've prayed, God knows I have, but my prayers don't seem to be accomplishing much."

When Eva bowed her white head, David quickly followed her example. "Holy Father in Heaven, I humbly request that You direct David in the pathway You have for him. Give him the wisdom and strength to do Your will. Please enable him to see Veronika with Your eyes and to seek her good. Help him to be patient and to trust You. Thank You for hearing this prayer and answering appropriately in Your time. We, your humble servants, pray this in the name of the Father and the Son and the Holy Ghost. Amen."

David raised his head. The strain had eased from his face; unutterable weariness was all that remained.

Eva quickly suggested, "Perhaps—would you like to rest in our guest chamber until time for Fellowship?"

David agreed with a sigh and "Yes, please," and when Eva peeked in through the slightly open door about fifteen minutes later, he was sleeping soundly, his head resting on a yarrow and lavender herb-laced pillow. She smiled to herself; God sent David to her to be ministered to in more ways than one.

As Eva tiptoed away, frantic tapping on the front door sent Eva hurrying to open it so the noise wouldn't disturb David.

Discovering Veronika standing on the stone step, gazing at her through red-rimmed eyes, Eva's mouth sagged for an instant as the thought passed through her mind that God had outdone Himself in sending a speedy answer to her prayer. But she quickly pressed her lips together and dismissed the idea; Veronika looked decidedly upset and there was very little time to pursue the reason before guests would begin arriving. With a soft greeting, Eva hastily drew Veronika inside and eased the door shut.

She took the girl by the hand, intending to guide her to the kitchen, where their conversation would not disturb David in the guest room located directly off the entrance hall. But Veronika didn't give her time—she immediately burst into tears and struggled through an emotional explanation of her distress.

Eva wrapped the distraught girl in her arms, hoping her motherly shoulders would absorb some of the sound.

"*Dívčí, dívčí, dívčí.*" She murmured the endearment over and over, as if repeating it would soothe Veronika's nerves. But when that failed to calm her torrent of tears, Eva just held her close and let her cry.

* * *

The sound of erratic tapping woke David out of a deep sleep, and it took him a minute to remember where he was. Ah, yes. He was in the Jamikovi's guest room. And the tapping was someone knocking on the front door.

David sat up and threw off the duvet as he swung his feet to the wool rug beside the bed. He stood up, fully intending to step out and make his presence known. But when wild sobs struck his ears, he sank back down on the bed, wondering who could be in such distress. And then, when he heard Veronika's voice, he couldn't make himself cover his ears.

"I don't know what to do," Veronika's words broke through her sobs. "I just can't face him every day for the next two weeks. It's hard enough here at Fellowship and on Sundays, but every day is more than I can bear." Further weeping muffled her ragged voice. "I haven't s-slept for days . . ."

David heard Eva question her, "Tell me, who are you talking about, *Dívčí?*"

"Why, it's David, of course," Veronika burst out, crying harder. "He'll be at the b-boarding house all day every day. I'll have to see h-him, and I . . ."

David fell back against the bed, suddenly physically ill. Veronika didn't love him; in fact, she struggled just to be around him. Well, he'd not bother her any more if that was how she felt. He'd been so sure Veronika was the one for him—but love had to be mutual. Unwilling to hear any more, David stuffed his fingers in his ears and waited for what seemed forever.

* * *

When Veronika had calmed enough to listen, Eva held her away and tactfully expressed her curiosity. "Perhaps I've been mistaken, but I thought you and David had taken a fancy to each other."

Shaking her head, Veronika confessed the source of her anguish. "Oh, Eva, I love David. I've tried not to, but I can't seem to help myself. But I'm not the kind of girl he'd choose to marry. I have no station. No money. Nothing. And anyway, he's going to marry someone else." Her tears started flowing again.

Startled, Eva frowned and questioned her intently, "You're certain about that?"

"Why, yes," Veronika asserted positively. "The girl and her mother came to see David while he was ill. It was my turn to sit with him, so I visited with them. When I asked what relationship they shared with David, the mother told me he was going to marry her daughter." She swiped at her teary eyes and sniffed.

"Hmm," Eva puzzled aloud. Something was definitely wrong here.

"Anyway," Veronika continued between sniffles, "I've tried to be his friend. This past S-Sunday morning was perfect—but I could hardly enjoy it, knowing we could n-never be more than friends. And then on our way here, he th-thanked me for helping him discover the reality of his f-faith. He got so excited he hugged me—lifted me right off my f-feet and whirled me around." Her hands flew up to cover her heart. "I-I thought I would die."

Her confession spilled out like a dam bursting. "He-he smelled so good. And I wanted him to k-kiss me. I wanted to kiss h-him!" She dropped her head in maidenly shame and finished in a whisper. "I couldn't even act h-happy for him. I was afraid if I sh-showed any emotion at all, I'd l-lose my self-control and betray my f-feelings."

She flung out her hands. "And then what could he do—feel s-sorry for me? I'd have put him in an awkward position. And I'd have lost what l-little relationship I do have . . ." she sniffed again and corrected herself, "what I d-did have."

Veronika clapped her hands to her wet cheeks, "Now I can't even have that; I can't b-bear being near him, l-loving him, and being teased with what I c-can never have." Her wail ended in a sob, "Oh Eva! I'm such a mess."

Eva rocked her in comforting arms until she grew quiet.

"Come to the kitchen with me, *Dívčí*." Eva raised her voice, hoping David was awake and had overheard Veronika's confession.

Drawing in ragged breaths as she scrubbed the remaining moisture from her cheeks, Veronika stumbled after Eva, following her to the kitchen at the back of the house. When Veronika was finally resting in a chair with her cold fingers wrapped around a mug of hot cider, Eva excused herself, intending to check on David.

Upon finding the guest bed rumpled but empty, Eva headed for the parlor. As she rounded the corner, she saw David's silhouette, a dark outline against the parlor window.

In response to Eva's footsteps, David turned toward her, volunteering, "I overheard." He swung abruptly back to the window, adding, "God certainly didn't waste any time answering your prayer!"

Unaware of David's misunderstanding, Eva felt confident that the situation would soon be happily resolved. She hurried back to the kitchen, where she found Veronika slumped in the chair, her head nodding sleepily. Eva rescued the mug and helped her guest to her feet.

When she'd led Veronika to the guest chamber, she plumped up the pillow to activate the herbal effects and then tucked the duvet around the girl's slim form—resting in the exact place where David had slept only a short time ago. Eva wagged her head, chuckling under her breath at God's sense of humor.

She slipped away to fetch an herbal compress for Veronika's tear-swollen eyes, but by the time she returned, Veronika was already asleep.

Firm knocking announced folks arriving for Fellowship, and this time Eva hurried to answer the door before the thumping woke Veronika. She held her finger to her lips in a signal to be quiet as Boris and Helina entered, followed by Tomas and Milan.

Everyone moved into the parlor before they began visiting, but Helina was uncharacteristically quiet and scarcely smiled. As soon as there was a break in the arrival of guests, she drew Eva aside.

"Veronika always walks with us, but when we stopped by the Karska's this evening, Jana said she hadn't come home for dinner. We are worried about her."

Eva didn't feel at liberty to betray Veronika's confidence, but neither did she want Helina to worry. "Hmm. I saw her earlier today. Something probably came up," she murmured in what she hoped was a reassuring tone.

Helina frowned. "I noticed David isn't here either. Do you suppose . . . could she be with him?"

Eva looked around in surprise. In the rush of welcoming folks, she hadn't noticed David's absence.

* * *

The sporadic knocking on the door combined with the sounds of conversation drifting from the parlor woke Veronika. For a few minutes she remained still, listening to the hushed greetings of arriving guests.

When the foyer was finally quiet, she got up. After hastily smoothing her hair and straightening her clothing, Veronika hurried to the parlor. Pale and silent, she slipped into a chair by the door just as the meeting began.

At the conclusion of the evening, Veronika hugged Eva and thanked her for her kindness before heading home with Boris and Helina. Immediately, Helina questioned her about her whereabouts, but Veronika demurred, saying something had come up to delay her, so she'd gone directly to the Jamikovi's from work.

Boris remained silent, loping along behind Veronika in brooding silence. Since he'd been back from helping his uncle, the three of them had resumed their old routine of walking to and from the Thursday evening meeting.

Veronika hadn't had an opportunity to speak to Boris alone, but since there had been no repeat of his strange, possessive behavior, she'd rethought the situation. From childhood, Boris had been an enigma—moody, withdrawn, and often fixated on a person, an object, or a routine. He'd said he liked smelling her hair . . .

Veronika finally concluded that she had misinterpreted his proprietary behavior as some kind of unrealistic romantic interest when he would likely behave in the same territorial way if he perceived a threat to his sister—or if Helena infused her washing water with sweet-smelling chamomile!

CHAPTER ELEVEN

"Fire! Fire! Come quickly!" Two wide-eyed, panting, gasping students burst into the university commons on Friday afternoon. "Come quickly! We need your help!" Shouting the alarm, the two messengers managed to enlist a following of would-be volunteers.

Crossing the Stone Bridge and racing up the hill, the growing crowd shouted to everyone they passed. "Help! Fire in Old Town. Bring your buckets. Come! Help us! Fire! Fire! Join us. Bring your buckets. We need your help! Fire!" And so it went as they dashed along the streets toward the fire.

David joined the volunteers, who along with the curious and the thrill-seekers, raced toward the bridge in response to the call. He could see the black smoke plume spiraling into the sky from the upper area of Lesser Town. Concern for the Karska's safety and for Veronika's home made him push through the crowd and sprint ahead. By the time he got near enough to see the flames, his nose burned with the acrid smell of smoke and his heart hammered loudly in his chest—and not just from the uphill sprint.

Angry, crackling tongues of fire shot out of the windows and through the doorways, devouring the three dwellings already engulfed and licking at the edges of a fourth. The fire was only five houses up the street from the Marenkova's and ten houses above the Karska's.

Stifling a cough from the smoke, David looked around, shrewdly assessing the situation. At the top of the hill, clusters of folks—worried-faced women, raggedly-clad children, and bent-backed elderly people—gathered in the street, intent on guarding the few possessions they'd managed to drag to safety. Feather pillows, cooking pots, bins of apples and nuts, and a wide assortment of household goods were tumbled in disorganized heaps on the cobbles. Grasping an obviously stolen raw joint of beef in his mouth, an enterprising dog snarled to frighten away several other mangy rivals.

Like ants, the hill's more able residents frantically carted chairs, tables, and bed frames from dwellings in the line of fire. Small children wailed, clinging to adults or older siblings, increasing the tension and hampering efforts to salvage family property. Chickens squawked and flapped about, adding to the general chaos. An elderly couple shuffled along the street, weeping and clutching each other as if they were lost.

When it became apparent to David that no one had given any thought to ending the tragedy, he began shouting to people, instructing them to form a bucket brigade from the river to the fire line and back to the river. Volunteers quickly responded, falling into serpentine lines, their backs bending first to the right and then to the left as each person reached for a bucket and passed it to his neighbor.

"You're doing a good job," David called out affirmation to the workers all along the brigade. "Keep up the good work."

When he was confident that the bucket lines could function on their own, he worked his way back to the thin lathe and plaster dwellings that simply melted in the flames.

Noting six hearty looking fellows who arrived too late to serve in the bucket brigade, David enlisted their help. Following his brief directions, they dismantled the house standing next in the fire's path, establishing a break in the row of wooden structures that shared side walls and sat like tinderboxes. By eliminating new fuel for the fire, the flames burned out when they reached the foundation stones where the dismantled house had stood.

One of David's fellow students, observing David's quick thinking and brilliant leadership capabilities, shouted his affirmation, "Good job, Da-vid!"

The volunteers on the bucket brigade picked up the cry and began yelling over and over, "Da-vid. Da-vid. Da-vid." Their sing-song chant grew in volume and intensity, until it reverberated across the river and could be heard all the way to Old Town square.

Invigorated by success, the volunteers shouted even louder and moved the buckets along at a faster rate. After about an hour of hard work, smoldering rubble was all that remained of the fire.

Praise for David spread through the crowd like the flames had spread along the street only minutes before. One by one, bystanders and volunteers turned their gaze to David, hailing him as the hero of the hour. Cheers escalated until the din of chanting drowned out all other sound.

Before he knew it, David found himself raised on the shoulders of strangers. Whooping and yelling as they lifted him high, the crowd of volunteers swarmed down to the river, across the bridge, and all the way back to the university.

* * *

News spread quickly through the shops and guilds. When facts mingled with postulations and exaggerations reached the boarding house, anxiety filled Veronika's heart. But work took precedence over worry; she could not leave to check on the Karska's status or that of their home.

When an excited student, reeking of smoke, returned to the boarding house bursting with his personal account of David's heroism, Veronika was reminded of how wrong she'd been in her original misjudgment of his character, and she whispered a prayer requesting forgiveness for her self-righteousness.

Several other students arrived and contributed their observations of David's intervention. By the time she left for home that evening, the smoke had dissipated and Veronika had a fairly comprehensive picture of the day's events. But Antonin and Jana had their first-hand experiences to relate, so she remained silent as they eagerly interrupted each other with details, proclaiming heartily the praises of

167

one so young who'd managed to save homes and lives by his quick thinking.

At last they were both quiet, having told and retold the day's events. It was then that Veronika spoke, her words dropping like pebbles into a pool. "David is my friend from the university who's been attending Fellowship and Sunday services at Bethlehem Chapel."

For once in her life, Jana Karska had nothing to say.

CHAPTER TWELVE

Church bells rang out jubilantly from the snow-tipped towers of St. George's Basilica. Clumps of bundled-up carolers, sporting rosy cheeks and broad smiles, brightened the busy streets and market squares with their merry voices. Candles burned in every window. The scents of winter greens and freshly baked sweets mingled in the air.

It was Christmas Eve, and it seemed that everyone in Prague, from the lowly to the great, was celebrating the birth of the Christ Child.

The Karska's were no exception; for the past week, Jana had busied herself with special baking. Oh, not like she did when she was a younger woman— but still, special treats stood in a row on her counter: nine-strand braided *vanocka* speckled with raisins, honeyed gingerbread, and nutty *vosi hnizda*.

Jana had brushed down her best gown of brown wool and she'd spot-cleaned Antonin's old black cloak until both garments could pass as respectable again. And Veronika's new *cotte*, delivered by Eva to the Karska home earlier that day, now hung on a hook near the girl's bed, ready and waiting to lend its beauty to her youthful grace.

Veronika's footsteps lagged as she crossed the bridge on her way home from At The Stone Swan. Certain she smelled snow in the air, she clutched the edges of her cloak in her fist to protect her against the cold and struggled to blink back her tears. She felt too tired to look forward to the midnight Mass at Bethlehem Chapel. A celebration at the Jamikovi's home for the members of their Fellowship would follow the service, but it had already been a long day and she ached for her bed.

Then, as she neared the Karska's home, the candle's light shining through the window reached out to lift her weariness. Inexplicably invigorated, she lifted her chin and hurried the last few steps.

The tantalizing aromas of mint, ginger, and yeast bread met her when she opened the door, reminding her that she'd been too busy to eat since breakfast.

"Oh, Jana, everything smells wonderful," she exclaimed.

"Well, come now and sit down. Our meal is quite ready and you must be hungry. Tuck a bite in you now, and then we'll be hurrying to go."

Raising her voice, Jana called her husband, "Come, Antonin. She's here."

As they settled into their accustomed places, Veronika drank in the anticipation on the faces dearest in the world to her. Lucas Jamikovi had offered to fetch them in his carriage so the elderly couple could attend the service. Veronika felt a surge of gladness for them—and for herself; it would be wonderful to ride.

When they'd finished their hasty meal of bean and mutton stew seasoned with mint and a bit of salt, Jana trailed Veronika to her curtained-off room.

"This morning Eva brought by a Christmas surprise for you. I hope you won't be minding that I rearranged your things so we could hang it on a peg." The older woman's voice shook with excitement. "Hurry now. It's been all day I've waited for you to see it, and I can hardly bide a minute longer."

In a surge of curiosity, Veronika pushed aside the curtain surrounding her partitioned space. Her eyes darted to her garment pegs. All it took was one glance at the lovely new gown, and the tears she'd held back earlier overflowed.

"Why, Roni, what you crying about? Put it on, *Dívčí*, and let's be having a look."

171

"It's too beautiful," Veronika whispered, blinking away the moisture that beaded on her lashes. "I felt so tired I didn't want to go tonight, but God is always doing things to let me know He cares. I am ashamed for allowing myself to be discouraged." Her slender fingers traced the lace-trimmed square neckline of the most beautiful gown she'd ever owned.

"Of course He cares," Jana stated matter-of-factly. "He's always busy looking ahead, if we'll just be trusting Him." She turned to go. "Hurry now—and come out and show yourself before you don your cloak."

Veronika poured chamomile water from the pitcher into the basin, inhaling deeply of the sweet scent as she quickly washed her face and hands. She removed her stained apron and her work *cotte* and slipped the rich blue silk gown over her head.

The long sleeves hugged her arms and ended in lace-edged points on the backs of her hands, the bodice molded her feminine curves, and the elegant fabric imparted a regal air.

With a caressing movement, she smoothed her hands over her narrow waist and slid them down over her gently rounded hips. It was amazing how such a generous and thoughtful gift could lift her spirit!

She removed her head covering. Her hair combs came out easily, and she grabbed up her boar-bristle brush and began brushing her golden curls.

As she rhythmically stroked the glossy strands, her mind strayed to David. She hadn't seen him since the Sunday visit to St. Vitus's Cathedral—but she had wondered about him with every other thought. What was he doing? Why wasn't he at the boarding house? Had he traveled to his home— where was his home? Would he be back when school resumed?

She knew Miss Merta had not been servicing his room, and none of the other maids or servants had commented on his absence. Not that she'd asked, of course. Everyone—students and hired help alike—told and re-told stories of his bravery, which made him seem bigger than life. And made it impossible to put him out of her mind. By the week's end she'd decided that missing him was far worse torture than facing him every day.

What she didn't know was that Lucas had hired David on a short-term basis to call on clients with outstanding debts for work done on wagons, carts, carriages, and wheels. Eva, hoping to give Veronika some space, had invited David to stay with them, and he'd accepted with pleasure. David never mentioned the Thursday he and Veronika had both visited Eva, and although decidedly curious, Eva refused to pry.

When it came time to leave to collect the Karskas in his carriage, Lucas, still busy helping his wife finish preparations for their anticipated guests, asked David to go instead. And although David would have preferred to decline the request, he couldn't refuse Lucas without an embarrassing explanation.

When David pulled the carriage to a stop in front of the Karska's home, Jana, watching at the window, opened the door before he could rap the knocker.

* * *

Veronika called out "Look, Jana!" as she flung open her curtain, twirling around so the fully gored skirt of her new *cotte* bloomed out around her.

Mid-twirl, her gaze landed on David, entering the front door. So shocked that she swayed, staggered, and almost fell, Veronika clutched desperately at the arm of the settee as she sank down on it. Agony boiled up and out in one hot, choked word.

"David!"

* * *

The partitioning curtain was flung back as a slender whirlwind of joyful abandon danced into the room, spreading a wave of tantalizing scent. David gasped, paralyzed by the painful longing that gripped his chest. His bright blue eyes—flames in his pale face—devoured Veronika. Never in his life had he been given such a vivid demonstration of what his selfishness had cost him. Dear God, hadn't he suffered punishment enough for his arrogance?

* * *

Jana's gaze took in Veronika's burning face and wide, tormented eyes. In the next heartbeat, her glance fell on David. Seeing the anguish that ravaged his expressive face, her breath caught in a sharp hitch.

But before she could speak, Antonin shuffled into the room from their tiny bedroom. Oblivious to the maelstrom of emotions engulfing its occupants, he commented, "Roni, Jana says you have a new *cotte*."

175

All eyes turned toward him, as if each person sought escape from the intense situation. However, due to his failing eyesight, Antonin remained blind to David's presence. Squinting at Veronika, the old man beckoned with a gnarled hand, "Come—over here— in the light, Roni. So I can see you."

Called out of her daze, Veronika slowly rose from the bench, her long curls loosely caressing her shoulders and gleaming like spun gold in the candlelight. With her eyes fixed on Antonin, she moved toward him like a sleepwalker.

When she stopped in front of him, Antonin reached out and clasped her shoulders in a gentle grip. "My, but you do look as beautiful as a bride."

Jana choked down her dismay at her husband's unwittingly tactless remark. Veronika's face blanched to the color of first milk. David shot to his feet.

In response to the movement, Antonin's faded eyes swerved to David. "Oh! I didn't see you there, Son. Did you come for us? Sorry to keep you waiting."

He squinted, glancing around the room. "This is my wife, Jana," he nodded toward the petite older woman. And then, before anyone realized Antonin's intent, he turned Veronika to face David—there was no escape—and said proudly, "and this is our Veronika."

Repressed emotion burned in a scarlet flush over Veronika's cheeks.

Unable to speak, David nodded. His hands balled into fists and his eyes burned like two black coals in his colorless face.

Jana broke in, a touch acerbically, "They've already met, my dear." She snatched up her cloak and thrust it toward her husband in a desperate effort to distract everyone. "Please, be helping me. We must go or we'll be late."

Veronika seized the opportunity to disappear behind her curtain, mumbling that she had to put up her hair.

In the safety of her private space she cupped her cheeks in her shaking palms. *Bože můj!* Could she plead sudden illness? She certainly felt wretched enough to do so honestly!

But how could she disappoint Antonin and Jana? She knew she couldn't; they had anticipated this evening for months.

God, help me! Veronika's frantic plea for courage was cast heavenward as she quickly twisted her hair into its usual simple style and ruthlessly stabbed in the combs to hold it in place. Sucking in a deep, shuddering breath, she stiffened her back, lifted a shaking hand, and by sheer will forced herself to push aside the curtain.

One swift glance revealed that Antonin and Jana were already out the door, moving slowly, supporting each other as they made their way to the carriage.

But David stood by the table, holding out her cloak.

Veronika fixed her gaze on the open doorway and held her breath as David swung the garment around her shoulders. But when the warmth of his touch unexpectedly brushed her neck, tears prickled behind her eyes and a tremor raced through her body. She clenched her teeth and swallowed a groan. She would be strong! She would make it to the carriage without falling apart!

As Veronika emerged from the house into the moonlight, Helina's breathless voice called from the dusky shadows up the street, "Wait! Wait for me. I'm coming."

In the throes of emotion, Veronika had forgotten that Helina had arranged to ride with them to the

Jamikovi's, where she would join Jana and Veronika in assisting Eva with last-minute preparations for their Fellowship's celebration meal to follow the midnight Christmas Mass.

Startled by Helina's call, the horses snorted and pawed impatiently, their moist, warm breath turning into frothy vapor in the cold air.

"Whoa, whoa," David's low voice soothed them as he darted toward the carriage, arriving in time to assist first Jana and then Antonin into the carriage.

As he swung around to aid Veronika, Helina rushed up, intercepting his move. With innate chivalry, David greeted her and grasped her elbow to help her inside.

When Helina was safely seated, David turned toward Veronika, his open palm extended. She stared at his bare hand and tentatively reached out her cold fingertips—how was it they had both forgotten their gloves? His lean, strong fingers closed over her smaller ones, and when he impulsively squeezed them, her eyes involuntarily flew to his. Even in the shadowy darkness, she couldn't prevent the surge of emotion that blazed in her eyes before she bit her lip and dropped her gaze to their hands.

* * *

Veronika's momentary, unguarded reaction sent inexplicable hope pounding through David's veins. In that instant he decided he had nothing to lose by pursuing Veronika. The whole world could think him a hero, but only one opinion really mattered. Hers. And he would not give up until she told him to his face that she could never care for him. And even if the end should prove to be a bitter one, he would know he had done all he could to win her.

Antonin leaned forward and peered around his wife, calling out, "Do you need some help, Son?"

"No, thank you. Things are fine, just fine," David tore his eyes away from Veronika and looked up as he reassured the old man. With squared shoulders, he handed Veronika into the carriage and then climbed up to sit on the driver's bench. At his signal, the horses moved the carriage forward. His merry whistle mingled with the clacking of the wooden wheels as they rolled over the frozen cobbles.

* * *

Inside the carriage, Jana and Helina exchanged greetings and shared their mutual excitement for the upcoming service and celebration to follow. But

Veronika remained silent, awash with conflicting emotions. She hadn't seen or heard from David in almost two weeks. Knowing the situation was best left alone didn't diminish her pain, nor could it squelch her heart's exuberant leap at seeing him again.

Her joy, however, was short-lived; David began to whistle a cheerful tune. He's obviously happy with his life; he hasn't missed me at all, she thought sadly. She let her head fall back against the carriage cushion and closed her eyes against Jana's worried look.

* * *

Boris paced angrily, recalling Helina's announcement as she prepared for the midnight service. "Veronika seems quite taken with David Branden."

He had grunted dismissively, but his sister didn't stop talking. "There'll be a wedding come spring, mark my words," she'd added, smugness lacing her prediction.

Boris had spun on his heel and shot out the door into the darkness, slamming the door behind him. For almost an hour he had paced up and down the street, kicking at cobblestones, breathing fire, and cursing every time he thought of Veronika with David Branden.

When the Jamikovi's carriage rumbled up the dark street, Boris lifted his head. Carriages were rare, and Helina had said he could go early and ride with them. But when he saw David Branden jump down from the driver's bench, anger rose like bile in his throat; he would walk rather than ride with him!

In the next moment, the Karska's door flew open, and he heard Jana invite David inside. So! The rich boy was welcome in their home. Hero, indeed. Anybody with any sense could have put a stop to that fire; he could have done it if he'd been there.

Boris continued pacing, wondering what was taking them all so long to come out and get in the carriage.

When Helina dashed out the door of their home and darted past him, her breathless call diverted his thoughts, "Wait! Wait for me. I'm coming." He stopped pacing, watching her run down the hill.

Although hidden in the shadows, Boris was close enough to see David assist Jana, Antonin, and then Helina into the carriage. When David extended his palm to Veronika, she put her hand in his. They hesitated, sharing what appeared to be an intimate glance.

Boris swore under his breath. Veronika belonged to him! He'd had his eye on her long before David came along, so he had first claim. That David Branden was a sneaking weasel. A predatory varmint. And he'd like nothing better than to skin him alive!

The carriage departed, leaving the street in silence. Boris resumed his agitated pacing while his tormented mind plotted obsessively.

* * *

Veronika heard Jana's low cry as they entered the door of the Jamikovi's home. *"Bože můj, Bože můj,"* Jana moaned her dismay as she stopped abruptly with her hands clutched to her heart.

Instantly alarmed, Veronika curled her arm around Jana's shoulders and begged in a tone bordering on panic, "What is it, Jana? Do you not feel well?"

"No. No. I'm just feeling a mite foolish now, that's it." The older woman shook her head and struggled to smile. "I clean forgot my *vanocka* at home."

Last to enter the house, David overheard Jana's distraught explanation. His offer was immediate, "I'll go back for it, *Pani* Karska. Just tell me what I should look for."

Relief flooded Jana's distressed face, "Oh, would you—but wait, I'll go with you. That would be best, now wouldn't it?" Resignation and disappointment suffocated the light from her eyes and the life from her voice.

Even as Jana spoke, Veronika knew she could never let her go. "No, Jana, you stay here; I'll go. It's no trouble for me. And then you can enjoy your visit with Eva before we leave for the chapel."

She moved quickly to the door, imploring David with an eloquent look and a rapid jerk of her head to come quickly before Jana's sense of duty could interfere with the long-anticipated pleasure of her evening out.

David patted Jana on the shoulder and spoke firmly, "We'll take care of it. Now, you go on in and visit with Eva. We'll be back before you know it." He gave her a slight nudge toward the Jamikovi's parlor. When she took a second step forward on her own, he dashed out the door after Veronika.

Anxious to be off, Veronika did not wait for David to help her into the carriage; she had one foot on the step by the time he joined her.

"Come, ride up on the bench with me." He flashed her a mischievous grin. "I know it's unconventional—but it's much more fun!"

Veronika hesitated, indecisive for a fraction of a second. Then she lowered her foot and moved to the front of the carriage. Her thoughts raced: What did she have to lose? Could the pain possibly get any worse? Would it be terribly wrong to enjoy the moments as they came?

David offered his hand, and when she took it, he deftly swung her up to the bench. Her heart pounded in her ears and her sharp breaths made smoky, white puffs in the frosty air.

"Thank you so much for driving me back to the house," Veronika hurried to say. She shivered and pulled her hands inside her cloak to keep them warm. "It means so much to Antonin and Jana to get to visit with Lucas and Eva. They almost never get out anymore."

"My pleasure. Besides," he said frankly, "I wanted a chance to talk to you." He glanced over at her. "I'm sorry I startled you earlier this evening. Lucas got caught up in helping Eva, so he sent me in his place.."

His matter-of-fact explanation smoothed the edge off her embarrassment. Forgetting her past heartache, Veronika smiled up at him, the joy of being with him momentarily eclipsing the pain it caused.

"I heard about the way you coordinated the volunteers at the fire. You were certainly brave. And very clever." Her comments precipitated a discussion that lasted until they arrived at the Karska's home.

David reined the team to a halt, then he jumped down and turned, reaching up to assist Veronika. As she bent her knees and stepped down, her left shoe slid on the icy step. With a sharp cry, she tumbled forward—straight into David's strong arms.

When he caught her against his solid chest, Veronika's heart nearly beat out of rhythm. With her nose pressed into his cloak, the smell of his sage soap filled her senses.

For an instant, she wished she was wrapped in David's arms because he loved her. But she knew she had forgotten to watch her step for looking at him— and as always, he was being a gentleman.

When David had steadied her on her feet, he lifted her chin with his curled hand and peered into her face. Concern laced his voice, "Are you all right?"

"Yes, but I feel so clumsy." Veronika's tremulous confession ended in a nervous laugh.

Grasping her hand, David squeezed it tightly in his large one and led the way to the house. He propped the door open with his shoulder and waited while she fumbled to light the candle kept just inside the door by touching the wick to the smoldering embers in the fireplace.

When the candle flickered to life, David stepped inside and pulled the heavy door shut. The sudden change in pressure sent a gust of cold air into the room, snuffing out the candle flame and plunging them into instant darkness.

Disoriented in the unfamiliar surroundings, David stumbled into the corner of the heavy oak table, sending its thick legs scraping against the floor. His shocked "Ouch!" was followed by a low chuckle as he rubbed his bruised thigh. "Now I'm the clumsy one. Maybe it would be best if I stay put and let you take care of things."

Playing on her already taut nerves, the chagrin in his voice and the awkwardness of the situation struck Veronika as funny. Laughter, unaffected and natural, bubbled up in her throat and escaped between her lips. After an instant of surprise, David joined in.

Unexpectedly, their shared spontaneous laughter in the anonymity of darkness released the tension between them. David laughed so hard he doubled over, leaning against the table and clutching his stomach, while Veronika laughed until tears ran down her cheeks.

As their chuckles finally faded, David recovered his sense of responsibility first. "Come," he gasped through a last chuckle, "we really must be going back."

Veronika immediately sobered. "Oh! Yes. Dear Jana will be worrying." She re-lit the candle and hastily collected the forgotten fruit bread. Its sweet aroma made her smile with anticipation. Life was good.

* * *

Clouds obscured the moon, so when a carriage and horses rounded the corner and started up the hill for the second time that evening, Boris, sidetracked from his anger, stopped pacing to listen. Two carriage visits to their street in one evening was startling enough, but when he saw that it was the same carriage returning again, he slouched his lumbering frame into the dark doorway of the house next to the Karska's, where he could see without being seen.

As the carriage drew close, his eyes bulged in their sockets and his growl swelled into a snarl. Veronika! What was she doing, sitting up on the driver's bench beside David Branden! Why, that was no place for a lady. What could the fool be thinking?

The carriage rolled to a stop near the Karska's front door, and Boris's thick brows tightened in an angry frown when David hopped down and turned to assist Veronika. But when she tumbled from the carriage step, falling into David's arms, Boris clenched his fists in outrage. His jealous mind told him that David held her much too close—and far longer than necessary. He smothered a vile curse and clenched his hands into fists.

As the unsuspecting pair entered the empty house, Boris crouched low and scraped along the wall. He came to a stop under the Karska's window and slowly raised his lanky body up the wall beside it. The single candle's flame produced very little light, which forced him to press his face to the glass and squint to make out the movement inside.

Suddenly, the light went out.

The table legs screeched on the wood floor.

And then a sharp, masculine "Ouch!" melted into peals of gasping laughter.

Even with his face pressed to the glass, Boris couldn't see a thing. But that didn't prevent his hate-twisted imagination painting vivid pictures for him of what was taking place between Veronika and David in that dark room.

While the passing seconds registered as minutes, Boris's rage escalated, blasting through his veins with such force that it fueled a rash determination to confront the pair.

But at that moment the candle flame flickered to life again.

Boris gasped and fell back, his bravado suddenly superseded by fear that he'd been caught spying— fear that for the moment was far greater than his hotheaded hostility and sent him fleeing back to the neighboring dark doorway.

Safely hidden in the shadows, Boris's panic died down. But his fury resurfaced as the Karska's house went dark a second time. Almost immediately the door opened and the two young people emerged.

Incensed, Boris watched through vicious, smoldering eyes as David took the towel-wrapped sweet bread that Veronika carried and then assisted her with his free hand as she climbed up to the driver's bench. When she was seated, he raised the bundle to her and then leaped up and sat beside her.

Leaning toward Veronika, David whispered something near her ear. Although Boris couldn't hear what was said, the intimate tone of Veronika's reply and the intimacy of their ensuing mingled laughter as the carriage rolled away torched his smoldering jealousy into all-consuming hatred.

* * *

By the time David and Veronika arrived at the Jamikovi's, it was time to depart for the midnight Christmas celebration at Bethlehem Chapel. Lucas joined David on the driver's bench after everyone else, amid much huffing and laughter, had managed to squeeze into the Jamikovi's carriage.

When the carriage came to a halt near the chapel in the square, Lucas jumped down and tied the horses to one of the many hitching posts stationed along the street. He helped his wife and Helina out on the right side while David assisted Jana and Antonin on the left.

The last to step down, Veronika deliberately kept her eyes fixed on the step. Falling into David's arms once was enough for one night.

"Oh, I do hope it snows tonight so we have a white Christmas," David whispered impulsively as he steadied her on the cold, uneven cobbles.

Veronika smiled up at his boyish enthusiasm. "Snow at Christmas always makes me think of why Jesus came."

Emboldened by her friendliness, David caught her hand and laced his fingers with hers as they followed their companions toward the chapel. "What do you mean?"

Veronika glanced down at her small hand enclosed in his large one. The warmth of his clasp made her heart ache and sent shivers down her spine. Her mouth went dry with emotion.

Tentatively wetting her lips, she admitted, "Well, Jesus came to make our sins as white as snow, so it wouldn't feel like Christmas to me without it."

As she spoke, David smiled down into her shining face. She met his glowing eyes with a sparkle in her own.

Side-by-side, they moved into the chapel and genuflected in acknowledgement of Christ's presence. They found two seats together several rows from the front on the right side and were barely seated before Brother Henrik began the processional.

"Mmmm." David heard Veronika draw in a slow, savoring breath—as if the familiar scent of the sacramental incense helped her open her heart to God's presence. Inspired by her reverence, he focused on the choir, his heart rejoicing at the words to the hymns they sang. And then as Brother Henrik read the verses from the Messianic psalms, he listened intently.

> *"The Lord said unto me: Thou art my Son,*
> *Today I have begotten Thee. Why do the*
> *nations conspire and the peoples plot*
> *in vain? Let the heavens rejoice and let*
> *the earth be glad before the face of the*
> *Lord, for He cometh."*

How had he missed the beauty and significance of the words he'd heard repeated year after year, he asked himself.

And then, too soon, the congregants stood for the final Christmas hymn.

> *Christ, redeemer of the world,*
> *Only begotten Son of the Father,*
> *Born ineffably of Him before time began.*

Thou art light, the splendor of the Father,
The eternal hope of all men; hear the prayers of
Thy servants throughout the world.

Recall, Author of our salvation,
How once thou didst receive our corporal likeness
And wast born of an all pure virgin.

The present day, brought back by the yearly cycle,
Attests to this; from the throne of the Father thou
Alone didst come down to save the world.

The heavens, the earth, the sea and all that is
Contained therein join together in a joyous
Canticle of praise for this day
Which marks thy coming.

We too, who are redeemed by thy precious blood,
Sing a new song on this day of thy birth.

Glory to thee, O Lord, who was born of a virgin,
With the Father and the Holy
Spirit, world without end. Amen.

A simple benediction brought the service to a conclusion, and immediately, the bustling crowd pressed into the aisles and surged toward the doors, anxious to enjoy the traditional after-Mass celebrating with food and fellowship in homes all over the city.

David blinked the moisture from his eyes and remained standing beside Veronika, oblivious to the movement around him. Venturing a quick glance her way, he saw that she too was unashamedly brushing away tears.

On impulse, Veronika turned to him. "It was—so beautiful." As more tears spilled down her cheeks, she gave a little apologetic half-laugh. But this time David smoothed them away, his fingertips lightly touching her face. As their dewy glance met and held, his hands dropped to her shoulders then slid down to clasp her upper arms.

How long would they have stood gazing into each other's souls, David wondered later, if Eva hadn't come looking for them. But the magic of the moment had to be set aside; Eva needed to depart at once to arrive home before her guests.

Joyce Brandt Williams

CHAPTER THIRTEEN

David and Lucas helped the occupants of the Jamikovi's carriage step safely to the ground before David hurriedly drove the carriage into the barn. He followed Lucas's directive to leave the team hitched to the carriage so it would be immediately ready to take the Karskas home after the celebration.

Entering the house ahead of everyone, Eva quickly slipped out of her cloak on her way to the kitchen, calling to the women and Antonin to deposit their belongings on the bed in the guest bedroom.

After divesting themselves of their winter wear, Helina and Jana hurried out of the room to help Eva, and Antonin shuffled after them, leaving Veronika by herself. She removed her own winter garments and placed them on the bed. Then pausing for a brief moment, she ran her hands over the smooth silk of her new *cotte*, delighting in its softness before she headed to the kitchen. She knew Eva would be busy, but thanking her for her thoughtfulness couldn't wait.

Jana and Helina were busily arranging food on the dining room table when Veronika hurried past them. Glad they had their backs to her, she slipped into the kitchen. Finding Eva bent over a large kettle, giving its contents a good stirring with a long-handled wooden paddle, she was suddenly overcome with gratitude.

Eva heard a choked cry and lifted her head. Seeing Veronika standing in the doorway, wearing the lovely blue *cotte*, she abandoned the wooden stirring paddle and crossed the room. "Do you like it, *Dívčí?*"

Veronika gulped and nodded; she still couldn't speak.

Eva motioned for her to turn around, and as she did, Veronika managed to find her voice. "Oh, Eva, I love it! It's the most beautiful *cotte* I've ever had! How can I ever thank you?" Throwing her arms around the older woman, Veronika impulsively kissed her on the cheek. Then suddenly embarrassed at her forwardness, she blushed and pulled back.

Meeting the girl's damp gaze with a secretive smile, Eva demurred, "Don't thank me, thank Him." She rolled her eyes heavenward. "It was His idea; I just do what He tells me."

With her next breath Eva changed the subject and resumed her responsibilities. "Now, *Dívčí*, would you greet the guests as they arrive? Collect their wraps and then direct the women to bring their food to the dining room."

Veronika's face beamed, "You know I'd love to!" Happy to show her gratitude, Veronika made her way to the front door.

* * *

No sooner had Veronika arrived in the vestibule, when the door opened and David stepped inside. In the light from the candles in the sconces in the entrance hall, Veronika's golden hair gleamed like a halo around her head. Her eyes were bright with happiness, and the threads in her blue silk dress shimmered with the rise and fall of her breathing. Speechless, David stared at her, so bemused he forgot to shut the door.

"Close the door, David. You're letting in the cold!" Helina called, coming up behind Veronika.

"What? Oh, yes, of course," David mumbled, tearing his gaze away from Veronika. He turned and pushed on the door.

Helina directed her attention to Veronika. "You look nice tonight. Is that a new *cotte*?"

"Ah, y-yes. Yes, it is," Veronika stammered a distracted reply before she moved forward to greet David.

"Come on in, David. Let me take your cloak," she said, extending her hands as David swiftly eased out of his heavy winter cloak. In the process of passing it to her, their fingers touched. Instantly, their eyes met and held as the tension between them escalated.

Staring at them speculatively, Helina cocked her head, raised her dark brows, and muttered under her breath with a satisfied smirk as she turned away, "You two are in a bad way!"

* * *

Within fifteen minutes the Jamikovi's house, festively decorated with pine boughs and candles, teemed with activity. Holiday treats, mulled cider, and creamed honeyed mead tantalized the senses and added to the gaiety of the celebration.

When it appeared that everyone had arrived, Lucas welcomed their guests in his unassuming way. He graciously bid them to enjoy each other's company and partake of the generous repast presented on Eva's long table.

Flushed and breathless, Boris arrived late for the celebratory meal. But no one noticed. Not that anyone ever noticed Boris. He was quiet and plodding, stolid and uncommunicative, and it would have come as a surprise to everyone who knew him that behind his quiet exterior a volcanic pressure was slowly building. Even at home, he kept his feelings to himself; an occasional grunt or growl summed up his everyday conversation. So long as Veronika was unattached, Boris was free to live in his imagination. But with the advent of David, it was just a matter of time before he erupted.

Boris posted himself in a corner, standing where he could observe the guests without entering into their conviviality. When he barely snorted an acknowledgement in response to Tomas's friendly nod and greeting, the widower moved on without giving him further thought.

Boris's black eyes fixated on David and Veronika, who were sitting in a corner. Intently engaged in conversation, they were oblivious to the world around them. Their obvious happiness exacerbated Boris's jealousy and gave legs to his hatred.

As the joyful evening came to an end, the women began clearing the food table. In the ensuing commotion as the guests sought out their host and hostess to express their thanks and collect their belongings, no one noticed that Boris quietly disappeared out the Jamikovi's front door.

Silent as a shadow, Boris propped his lanky body against the house and tasked his burning eyes with studying the departing guests. In the darkness, he waited, anger fueling his rash vendetta.

* * *

When nearly everyone had gone, David exited through the back door, whistling under his breath. He felt happier than he had in months.

In the stable, he spoke to the horses in soothing tones before he mounted the bench, snapped the reins, and resumed his whistling. He drove Lucas's carriage around to the front of the house to collect Veronika, Helina, and the Karskas.

When the team came to a stop, David bounded to the ground in a single leap. Still whistling softly, he tied the reins to a nearby hitching post.

Barely three steps from the door, a hand shot out of the darkness and roughly clamped onto David's arm. As the grip tightened, jerking David toward his unseen assailant, the attacker snarled, "Leave my girl alone, rich boy."

A hard fist struck David above the ear. Thrown off balance, his feet shot out from under him and his head smacked on the ice. Stunned, David squinted, trying to make out his assailant between the stars flying in front of his eyes.

Vitriol spewed out with each word. "I saw you, you weasel."

Clutching his head that screamed with pain, David was suddenly aware of hot, oozing moisture sticking to his hand. Blood! He gasped for air. "Wh-What are you talking about?"

His assailant barked another hate-saturated allegation." I heard you two laughing. In the dark."

David identified Boris's voice, but it took him a moment to make sense of the accusations. Then it dawned on him: Boris was Veronika's neighbor. When David had followed her into her home earlier that evening, Boris must have been watching. The candle had gone out and they'd laughed at David's clumsiness. But Boris's twisted, jealous mind had evidently imagined the worst.

David managed to scramble to his feet. He staggered and then straightened up."

With his fist raised for another assault, Boris ploughed forward, his low, venomous incrimination piercing the night like a dragon's breath. "You've ruined her!"

Enraged at the insult leveled against Veronika's character, to say nothing of his own, David's response was instinctive; his left arm came up, deflecting Boris's strike even as he delivered a powerful blow to his accuser's left jaw.

"Get your mind out of the moat, man. You dishonor her to even think such evil of her."

Although Boris staggered under the force of David's fist, he would have regained his balance if David hadn't followed the first blow with a second, more direct than the first.

Boris reeled and fell, sprawling awkwardly on his back on the frozen ground. David eyed him unsympathetically.

As Boris lay there cursing and groaning, covering his face and cowering as if he expected to be kicked, the indignation drained out of David. He shook his head in disbelief then grimaced in pain as he swung around and stomped heavily into the house.

Lucas and Antonin were engaged in conversation when David, blood trickling down the side of his face, abruptly interrupted them, blurting out his distress. "I-I've just been attacked—over someone's honor."" Jaws dropped and all eyes turned toward him as the guests still present in the Jamikovi's parlor stopped talking mid-sentence.

David's voice grew unsteady, "I-I defended myself . . . and I left him on the ground outside your front d-door. I think you need to make sure h-he's gone when I leave—or I'm a-afraid I . . ." he shuddered, "I might do him more harm."

In his slow way, Lucas inquired, "Well, now, David, whose honor was maligned that you came to blows?"

With a quick, nervous glance around the room, David tightened his jaw in stubborn resolve and dropped his eyes to the toes of his boots. "I'd rather not say."

"Stay here, my boy. I'll deal with—the situation." When Lucas turned on his heel and strode from the room, Antonin followed him, his shuffling gait resounding like a drum roll in the shocked silence.

David dropped into the closest chair and buried his blood-streaked head in his hands. Jana slipped her arm around Veronika's slender shoulders, and Hana, who'd been visiting with Helina, grabbed her hand in mutual support. Eva rushed to get a damp cloth to clean David's face, along with her jar of herbal salve to treat his wound. The remaining guests resumed quiet conversation, discreetly trying to ease the awkwardness.

Within a few minutes, Lucas and Antonin returned to the parlor. Again, conversations were suspended as everyone's attention gravitated toward Lucas. The big man strode across the parlor until he stood beside David, who had his eyes closed and was wincing as Eva gently cleaned the cut on his head. After she applied a compress to stop the bleeding, Lucas rested his hand on the younger man's shoulder. David opened his eyes but he didn't say anything.

Lucas's voice was low, but it was firm. "He has gone, David." Then looking around at the shocked faces of the gathered guests, Lucas suddenly realized they needed a brief explanation and David needed vindication. "I'm not much for violence, but in this case, I'd say it was warranted."

He squeezed David's shoulder in a reassuring gesture, and then surprised everyone who knew him as a mild-mannered fellow by making a bold statement, "I'm sure I'd have done the same thing myself."

The tension in David's shoulders visibly relaxed and a tremor ran through the length of his body. He pressed his lips together on a sigh and lifted his head to meet Lucas's sympathetic gaze. "Thank you. I've never hit anyone in my life. But Boris attacked—" He broke off abruptly when his eyes landed on Helina's stricken face; Boris was her brother. He wished he could take back his words, but it was too late.

Blindly turning away, Helina muttered painfully, "I must be going."

"Wait, everyone." Lucas immediately drew the attention away from Helina. "Please, no talk about this. When a soul hangs in the balance, we must pray for mercy."

Heads nodded. Then the few remaining guests quietly gathered their belongings and murmured subdued thanks and farewells.

When everyone had gone except David, Veronika, Helina, and the Karskas, Eva grasped her husband's arm. Securing his attention, she suggested, "Why don't *you* drive these folks home—and leave David here with me so I can take care of his wound."

* * *

A heavy silence filled the carriage. No one knew what to say. Helina was trembling and too upset to speak. Veronika sat stiffly in her corner, eyes closed and arms crossed over her chest. And Antonin and Jana floundered mentally—they had never faced anything like this.

When the longest ride of their lives came to an end, Helina managed a choked good-bye and jumped to the ground before Lucas could assist her. She dashed up the hill, disappearing in the shadows of the houses along their street.

With great effort, Veronika restrained her impatience, offering her arm to Antonin, who was unsteady on his feet in the best of circumstances. As they moved toward the door, she called out their thanks over her shoulder, while Jana rushed ahead to open the door and light the candle.

As soon as the three of them were safely inside, Antonin tugged Veronika around to face him. "Could I be having a word with you, Veronika?"

"What is it?" she mumbled. He always called her Roni, never Veronika, unless she was being called into question for her behavior. Her shoulders sagged. Even the warmth of home did nothing to relieve her heartache and weariness.

"Boris told Lucas that you and Mr. Branden came into our home this evening without a chaperone, and that Mr. Branden took liberties with you in the dark—and that you both were laughing."

Veronika's eyes widened and her mouth dropped open. "W-Why would Boris say that? He wasn't even here!"

"He said he was taking a walk earlier this evening when he saw you and Mr. Branden come into the house alone. He has an idea that you belong to him; he claimed you're going to marry him."

"What!" Veronika jerked free from Antonin's grasp. Her body grew rigid as she forced her protest through gritted teeth, "Never! Never, never, never. I could *never* marry Boris." She wrapped her arms around her middle to contain the sudden trembling that shook her body.

"And what about his accusation?" Ever patient, Antonin questioned mildly.

Emotionally stretched to the breaking point, Veronika burst into tears and flung out her hands in a defiant gesture. "It's not true! It's just not true! We did come back to get the *vanocka* that Jana forgot, but we didn't do anything wrong."

When neither Antonin or Jana made any response, Veronika suddenly realized that two worried faces were anxiously waiting for her further explanation.

Straightening her shoulders, she drew in a ragged sob and then huffed in sharp annoyance, "I lit the candle so I could see, but when David shut the door, the flame went out. It was so dark in here that David ran into the table."

She hesitated, recalling their shared laughter; this whole unfortunate situation had quickly tarnished the pleasure of those few special moments. Sucking in an edgy breath, she finished crossly, "I re-lit the candle and collected the *vanocka,* and we left. And that's all that happened. Honest."

When tremors shook Veronika's body again, Jana slipped her arm around the distraught girl and shot her husband a look that said, *Leave the poor girl alone.*

210

Antonin hastened to reassure her, "I believe you, Roni. I just wanted to hear—from you—what happened."

As Veronika turned away, he added, "'It was mighty good of that young Mr. Branden to defend your honor. You must be sure to thank him next time you see him."

Veronika's weeping bordered on hysterical, and Jana hurried her off to bed.

* * *

As soon as everyone had gone, Eva gently re-examined David's head. Determining that the bleeding had stopped and the cut was small, she skillfully applied a small bit of vervain ointment, one of her own formulations.

When she had finished, David heaved a weary sigh and shifted, leaning back in his chair.

Eva determinedly seized the opportunity fortuitously presented by the evening's events to speak to David about his relationship with Veronika.

"So, Boris insulted Veronika?" her mild question tactfully invited David's confirmation and comments.

David growled, "He accused us of—" his shoulders slumped, "—well, I'd rather not say."

Eva didn't comment, and they sat in silence for a moment.

Then David confessed, "The truth is, I feel as sorry for him as I've been feeling for myself."

"Sorry for yourself!" Eva's shock circumvented her usual diplomacy. "Why, whatever for? I thought after the Thursday when you and Veronika both came to see me, you'd be over the moon. Did something go wrong?"

Despite his pain, David's head snapped around to face her, his eyes glaring with naked reproach. "How can you even ask? Everything's been all wrong since!"

His tone grew more strident. "Why should I be happy to learn that the girl I love can't stand to be around me?" He bolted to his feet and began pacing back and forth like a prisoner in a cell while dragging his fingers through hair that already bore ample evidence of previous abuse.

Startled by his unexpected outburst, Eva scolded, "After you heard Veronika say she loves you, I thought you'd explain about that other girl—whoever she is."

As if struck by lightning, David froze mid-step. "What other girl?" he demanded hoarsely, his eyes burning in his colorless face.

Eva's voice wobbled uncertainly, "W-Why, the girl who came to see you while you were sick. Veronika said the mother told her you were going to marry her daugh . . ."

"That's what they thought?" David interrupted, wheezing in air like a suffocating man. He stood paralyzed for a long moment before his chin dropped and he turned away. He clutched his head and groaned into his hands. "How could I have been so blind?"

Then before the words were hardly out of his mouth, David whipped back around so suddenly that Eva nearly fell off her chair. His eyes bored into hers as he demanded, "Veronika loves me?"

"David," she reproached, astonishment shooting her voice up an octave, "of course she loves you." She sobered. "But you already know that. You overheard my conversation with her."

A confused frown replaced David's despair. "I don't understand. With my own two ears," he laid each palm along the sides of his face, covering his ears, "I heard her say it was bad enough to see me on Thursday's and Sunday's without having to face me every day!"

"Go on," Eva prompted. "What else did you hear?"

"N-Nothing. I couldn't bear any more." He squeezed his eyes closed on his memory. "I stuck my fingers in my ears and lay back down and waited."

The impish twinkle in Eva's eyes danced in her voice. "You poor boy. I'm afraid—oh, do forgive me if I laugh." She erupted in a hearty chuckle.

"I really don't see what's so funny," David barked, then winced as pain shot through his head.

"I-I'm s-sorry," she stuttered through her repressed her laughter. "It's just that the two of you have been miserable for nothing. Had you listened a bit longer, you'd have heard Veronika's reason for avoiding you in the first place." Eva covered her mouth in another effort to stifle her chuckles.

David's shoulders lifted and he took a hopeful step toward her. "And that is . . ."

"She's convinced her station in life is so far beneath yours that you would never consider marrying her."

His head jerked back. "She said that?"

"Oh, yes. And a lot more." Her gentle teasing exuded affection.

"Like what?" David demanded, striding across the room to stand over her. His flaming eyes bored into hers.

"Like the Sunday you took her to St. Vitus's Cathedral . . ."

"Yes?" The hope and despair that warred in his breast rose to his face.

"She said you hugged her. And that she wanted to kiss you—*desperately* wanted to kiss you. Those were her words—where are you going?" Eva sputtered as he spun away from her.

"To see Veronika, of course!" He flung the joy-filled words over his shoulder as he dashed out the front door.

* * *

David's determined pounding shook the Karska's house and rattled their only window. After a few moments, he heard Jana's anxious voice, "Answer the door, quick, before Roni wakes up. Oh, Antonin, who could it be? Not that horrid Boris, I'm hoping."

Antonin cracked the door open and peered out.

David stared back at him. Now that he was here, he was at a sudden loss for words.

As Antonin opened the door a bit wider, Jana edged into view. "What you be wanting, young man?"

Her beady eyes scrutinized him from head to toe and came to rest on the gash on his head that gleamed in the moonlight.

It suddenly dawned on David how terrified these two old people must be, awakened from very belated sleep and then finding him, bloody and disheveled, looming at their door, given his aggressive behavior earlier that night. But having come this far, he wasn't about to give up. "I must speak with Veronika."

"Do you know the time? You should be in bed," Jana rebuked him, pushing on the door.

"You are absolutely right, *Pani* Karska," David agreed, even as he impetuously stuck his foot out to hold the door ajar, "but I just couldn't wait until tomorrow."

"Wait 'til tomorrow for what?" Although Antonin sounded suspicious of David's motives—or his sanity, his nightcap had fallen askew and half covered one eye, giving him a droll appearance that offset the severity of his tone.

* * *

Startled by loud pounding on the door, Veronika raised her head off her pillow. She heard Jana's frightened voice and Antonin's shuffling footsteps.

And then there was the familiar creak as the front door opened. That voice—

Veronika vaulted out of bed. That was David's voice! What could he possibly want at this time of the night—no, morning?

In one swift movement, she discarded her nightgown. Catching up her new cotte from the peg where she'd hung it earlier, she pulled it over her head and jerked the laces.

Barefoot, her rumpled hair falling loosely down her back, Veronika pushed aside her curtain in time to hear David declare, "To tell her that I love her."

As shock spiraled down her spine, Veronika overheard Antonin's surprised stutter, "And th-that couldn't wait 'til tomorrow?"

"No. It couldn't! *Pani* Jamikovi just told me that Veronika thinks I'm committed to someone else. So I had to come, to tell her that it isn't true." His voice shook with his intensity. "I love Veronika. I want to marry her."

David's declaration propelled Veronika across the room. Turning sideways, she managed to slip between Jana and Antonin and emerge face-to-face with David. Backlit by the fireplace's golden glow, she could have passed for an angel.

"You love me? You really want to marry me?" her voice was soft with wonder.

"Most definitely!" David stated emphatically, reaching for her hands. "But I need to know ... do you love me?" His eyes bored into hers. "You've deliberately avoided me, so I thought you didn't like me."

Veronika hung her head and tried to explain. "I know you could—*should* choose someone closer to your station in life. I have no dowry. I don't even know who my parents were, David! So I tried to stay away. That's why I ..." her voice dropped to an agonized whisper, "why I lied to you—and caused all the trouble with Boris." Her eyes welled with remorseful tears, "I'm so sorry he hit you ..."

David's grip on her hands tightened, but he didn't interrupt.

Pressing her lips together, Veronika swallowed hard and continued, "And then, when *Pani* Bortskova came to see you while you were sick, she said they planned to announce their daughter's engagement to you by Christmas. So I traded the caring of your room with Miss Merta ... Oh, David, I was trying to do the right thing!"

David attempted a frown, but he ended up grimacing when the movement of his muscles caused him pain. "In hindsight, I can see that the Bortskova's hoped I would marry their daughter—but that was never my intent; I beg you to believe me." His earnestness was most convincing.

"I do believe you."

"But you still haven't answered my question . . ." his words vibrated with tension, "Do you love me?"

"Yes, David, of course I do. Love you." She gave a half sobbing little laugh. "With all my heart."

"All right then! And just so you know, now and forever, there is no one else for me. And I could care less who your parents were!" He pulled her tightly into his embrace.

At last she was where she longed to be, wrapped in David's arms. Oblivious to Antonin's and Jana's startled exclamations, David and Veronika forgot the world around them in a kiss that left no doubt in the minds of their witnesses that God meant them for each other.

When Veronika finally pulled away, gasping for air, half laughing, half crying, David drew her back.

With eyebrows raised, Antonin and Jana exchanged a startled glance. Antonin's face broke into a broad grin and he pulled Jana close, obviously not about to miss out on such a prime opportunity for a little romance.

Laughingly serious, Jana gave Antonin a smacking kiss before she pushed him away and turned to admonish David, "Either step inside, young man, or go home."

The young lovers parted, but their happiness bubbled up into joyous laughter. And when they had both calmed a bit, David, with one arm still around Veronika's shoulders, ran his fingers through his hair and tried to subdue his fatuous grin.

"So, what do you have to say for yourself? Antonin's question brought David up short.

Clearing his throat, David replied respectfully, "I'll be back tomorrow to ask properly for her hand."

"All right. See to it, Son."

David nodded, but his attention had already returned to Veronika. He held her away an arm's length, "Poor darling. I'm sorry I woke you."

Veronika's eyes never left his face as she reassured, "It's wonderfully all right, David. I'm so glad you came tonight and didn't make me wait until tomorrow." As her hand crept up to caress his cheek, she promised, "I'll never forget it."

David bent to kiss her again, gently at first, but when the kiss intensified, lasting to the point of embarrassment, Jana scolded, "Now, now. That's enough for one night. You may be a hero, but we have to live with our neighbors."

Reluctantly, the lovers drew apart.

Determinedly whisking Veronika inside, Jana turned her head and winked at David over her shoulder as she ordered, "Go home. Get some sleep. You can come back tomorrow."

"What time, *Pani* Karska?" He flashed her a disarmingly cheeky grin.

Always quick to think on her feet, Jana retorted, "When the goose is cooked!"

Joyce Brandt Williams

CHAPTER FOURTEEN

One year later.

Snowflakes floated down and settled with a whisper, clothing autumn's decay in magical white splendor. But to the two young people sitting together, their heads bent over the Bible in the Jamikovi's parlor, it could have been raining fire and brimstone and they probably wouldn't have noticed. Their love had grown and blossomed in spite of, or perhaps because of the obstacles they'd had to face.

In the early afternoon on Christmas Day one year ago, David had properly presented himself to Antonin and Jana Karska and formally requested Veronika's hand in marriage. When the older couple had heard each of them express their affection, they bestowed their approval. The four of them enjoyed a happy afternoon and celebrated the occasion by sharing a meal together.

The following morning David had paid a visit to Professor Bortskova and manfully apologized for inadvertently misleading his family. It was a humbling experience that David resolved never to have to repeat. The older man had graciously reassured David of his commitment to him and his education and tactfully suggested he discontinue joining the Bortskova family for Sunday evening dinners.

Helina had knocked on the Karska's door late Christmas morning to apologize for her brother's behavior and to inform Veronika and the Karskas that Boris had gone back to live with their uncle's family. Although they managed to work through the awkward conversation with their friendship intact, Helina chose not to tell them Boris had begged her to notify him if Veronika's reputation needed rescuing; she couldn't see any need for mentioning that after Veronika, her face beaming, had confided that David would be coming later in the day to properly ask Antonin for permission to marry her.

It had been over a year now since Antonin and Jana had given their approval and Veronika had said yes to David's proposal—but it was with a request: that David would instruct her in Latin so she could read the Bible for herself.

David hadn't wasted any time. He set out immediately to acquire a Bible, but he was quickly informed that it was against the law for an individual to own one. He was told the Scriptures were so difficult to understand that the common folk must be protected from reading and interpreting them in a heretical way.

David knew that Father Klemens, who served in the Chapel of the Shepherd at Burg Mosel since Father Andrej's death, possessed a Bible, but the good Father always took it with him because he also served the small parishes in several nearby villages on Branden land. Finally, with Brother Henrik's help and a letter from Father Klemens, David purchased a large, leather-bound, hand-written Bible by registering it for the Chapel of the Shepherd at Burg Mosel. Then he carefully instructed Veronika regarding its purpose, in the event that she should ever be questioned about the purchase.

Later, David asked Eva about the legality of the Bible that held pride of place in the Jamikovi's parlor. She informed him that Brother Henrik felt it would be "safer" in a home during weekdays than sitting in an empty chapel where someone could steal it. So he applied for and was granted official permission to "store" it. But every Sunday it was returned for use in the service at Bethlehem Chapel.

For the past year David and Veronika had spent each Sunday afternoon in Latin study, sometimes at the Karska's home, but most often in the Jamikovi's parlor where they had a measure of chaperoned privacy. With dedication and hard work, Veronika had progressed to the point where she could actually read most of the words in each sentence. Desire was a strong motivator, David was a patient teacher, and the two had persisted diligently.

Today, Veronika opened the heavy Bible resting on her lap to the marker in Genesis, to the story of Eleazar, Abraham's servant, sent to find a wife for his master's son, Isaac. With David, her husband of one week, seated beside her on the settee, she began reading where she'd left off last Sunday.

> *"And her brother and her mother said, 'Let the damsel abide with us a few days, at the least ten; after that she shall go.'*
> *And he said unto them, 'Hinder me not, seeing the Lord hath prospered my way; send me away that I may go to my master.'*
> *And they said, 'We will call the damsel, and*

enquire at her mouth.'
And they called Rebekah and said unto her,
'Wilt thou go with this man?'
And she said, 'I will go.'
And they sent away Rebekah, their sister, and
her nurse, and Abraham's servant, and his men.
And they blessed Rebekah, and said unto her,
'Thou art our sister, be thou the mother of
thousands of millions, and let thy seed possess
the gate of those which hate them.'
And Rebekah arose, and her damsels, and they
rode upon the camels, and followed the man: and
the servant took Rebekah, and went his way."

As Veronika read the account out loud, her pace slowed. She faltered, and then stopped altogether, staring at the page.

"Why did you stop? Do you need help with a word?" David offered, glancing at her.

With a shake of her head, Veronika whispered, "No, I'm not stuck." She raised wonder-filled eyes. "I just realized that I'm doing exactly what Rebekah did! I'm leaving Antonin and Jana behind, and I'm going with you to live in a strange place. And I don't know your family."

"Well, at least you know *me*," David quickly pointed out. "Rebekah had never met Isaac. For all she knew, he might have been contrary to her liking." He flashed her his most engaging grin.

Veronika returned his smile. "She really had to trust God. I'm glad He didn't ask that of me." She slipped the marker into place and closed the heavy leather Bible.

"Are your things all packed to leave in the morning?" David inquired.

"Yes. And Antonin and Jana are very happy in the servants' quarters here with Lucas and Eva. I don't know how I could have left them if a situation hadn't worked out for their care. Antonin is delighted that Lucas gave him some small jobs in his shop—he feels like he's earning his keep. And Jana is thrilled to be helping Eva with her herbs. God has been so faithful, and . . . oh, David, I'm so excited," a flicker of anxiety crossed her face as she impulsively admitted, "and a little afraid, too."

"Afraid of what, my love?"

"Ohhh," she drew the word out on a sigh, her eyes staring at an unnamed spot as she confessed, "I'm just a little afraid your family might not like me, might think I'm not right for you." She turned and looked him straight in the face with her fear.

"I doubt it," David reassured her. "But at least *I* like you; Rebekah didn't even have that consolation."

When she leaned forward to kiss him for his kind words, David pulled her close, breathing in her familiar chamomile scent as she rested her head on his chest.

A few minutes later, still wrapped in each other's arms, they were interrupted by Eva summoning them for the final evening meal together before their departure in the morning.

CHAPTER FIFTEEN

It was the last day of their journey to Burg Mosel. David and Veronika rose before dawn, determined to get an early start. David invited Veronika to join him in the great hall of the Red Deer Inn for breakfast, but she declined, admitting that she was much too nervous to eat.

While David was gone, Veronika washed her face and hands in the basin with water from the pitcher, scenting it with a few drops of chamomile oil from the bottle David gave her as a wedding gift. After donning the pretty blue silk cotte that she'd worn for Christmas Eve and for Sunday services since Eva had made it for her, she twisted her golden hair into a simple knot at the back of her neck and secured it with her combs.

When the last of their belongings had been sealed in their trunk, Veronika slipped into the ermine-trimmed black wool cloak Lucas and Eva had lavished upon her as a farewell gift. She pulled the matching ermine hat over her head and blinked away the unbidden mist that clouded her eyes as she thought about her dear friends, now so far away.

But there was no time to dwell on the past; David's rapid steps on the stairs pulled her attention back to the present.

"Are you ready?" he called, bounding through the door.

She turned to face him. "Yes, David, I'm ready." It was more than an answer; it was a promise.

When their trunk had been stowed in the sleigh and heavy wool blankets tucked in tightly around her, Veronika sat up very straight and looked apprehensively in the direction David had pointed last night when indicating their destination. Staring at the outcropping, now clearly visible in the morning light, her thoughts strayed back to the biblical account of Rebekah and her journey by camel to her new home.

"Why so serious, my love?" David questioned her anxious expression as he slid onto the bench beside her. "Are you still worried about meeting my family?"

"I was thinking about Rebekah," she answered, smiling at his undisguised boyish eagerness that reassured her without words that all would be well.

She knew he'd written to his parents after Christmas last year with news of their engagement and paid a courier to deliver his letter. He'd received a heartfelt note in return, sending their warmest congratulations. Then almost two months ago, David had written to tell them of his plan to be married at Christmas and that he would be bringing his new bride home after the new year. Although he didn't say much, she knew he was disappointed not to hear from them. But mail delivery was sporadic at best.

When David got excited, he talked, and today was no exception. He entertained Veronika with tales of his boyhood days, recalling pranks played on the servants; summers spent at Feste Burg, the family's primitive fortress on the Baltic Sea; playing games with the servants' children; sliding in stocking-covered feet on the polished great room floor—along with the caning he'd received when caught; sliding down the banisters in the entrance hall; and how his mother had found her way out of the secret chamber to warn his father of Jacques Monet's intent to murder him.

At the mention of Jacques's last name, Veronika's fingers, entwined with her husband's, twitched involuntarily. Abruptly, she pulled her hand away.

David's eyes immediately sought hers. "What's wrong?"

"I just had a horrible thought." She repressed a shiver. "I never knew my parents, but my family name is Monet." She worried out loud, "What if I'm related to that horrible Jacques person?"

"Not likely," David scoffed. "He was an evil, treacherous man, and you're the sweetest, dearest girl God ever made. Come now, don't let your imagination spoil our wonderful day." He reclaimed her hand and played with the little ring that had been her mother's, twisting it around and around on her slender finger.

As they crested a ridge and looked across the valley toward Burg Mosel perched high on the outcropping, they could see snow falling in the valley below while the sun shone brightly from above. The sunlight reflected off each frozen flake, filling the sky with glittering crystals; like twinkling stars, they floated down from heaven. Simultaneously, they caught their breath.

David whispered in awe, "It's a sign that God will bless our life, my Rebekah." He bent his head and sealed the promise with a tender kiss.

With each passing mile, Burg Mosel grew larger. By mid-afternoon David projected that within the hour they would begin the ascent up the steep trail leading to his home at the summit. He could hardly sit still for excitement, and his anticipation was infectious. Veronika's breathing quickened and her cheeks flushed pink with a feverish blend of eagerness and trepidation.

She silenced her anxiety with the fact that David was now her husband. Father Henrik had married them in a simple, sweet ceremony in the Jamikovi's parlor the day after David finished his studies at the university—one week before Christmas. Eighteen days ago, to be exact.

Burg Mosel loomed ahead of them now, standing out against the blue-gray sky. The ancestral mansion rose up as an obvious bastion of security for the many villages dotting the surrounding countryside, and a blue flag flew proudly from the peak of the tallest tower.

When the horses slowed as they began the ascent of the outcropping, Veronika closed her eyes and mouthed a silent prayer asking God for courage. David slipped an arm around her shoulders and pulled her close. She leaned her cheek on his chest, and he rested his chin on the top of her head.

As they passed between the heavy iron gates, David's arm tightened before he whispered, "We're here, my love."

Veronika straightened up and opened her eyes. And nearly fainted. The size and elegance of the stately residence surpassed even her wildest imaginings. Grand stone steps led up to the front entrance. Mammoth jardinières, bonneted with snow, rested on the corners of the stone balustrades. Massive double doors, faced with worked iron, were more intimidating than welcoming. And the guardian angels etched into the stone frieze topping the doors seemed to be staring straight at her—as if they knew she did not belong here.

Veronika stifled a gasp and shrank back against her seat.

When the sleigh came to a halt by the rear entrance, David leaped to the ground and nearly plucked Veronika out of the sleigh in his exuberance. Several stable boys instantly appeared to take care of the horses and a servant was dispatched to enlist assistance with their trunks.

David grabbed her hand and led the way to the entrance. He swung open the door and drew her into the vast entrance hall with its lofty, vaulted ceiling, sweeping staircase, massive chandelier, and intimidating collection of ancestors' portraits. She gasped, but David didn't give her time to worry about her humble origins; with a tug on her hand, he started across the marble floor.

They'd only taken a few steps when a short, plump, older woman emerged from the clerk's office. She took one look at them and her face blanched as white as her hair.

"Stop! Stop!" she shrieked wildly. Then she spun around and dashed away from them as if she were running for her life.

"What's gotten into Dagmar?" David wondered out loud, pulling Veronika after him as he ignored the housekeeper's puzzling behavior and followed the fleeing woman down the long corridor lined with paintings and tapestries.

David had talked about the ancestral home where he grew up, but his descriptions had not prepared Veronika for Burg Mosel's splendor. Or perhaps it was that her imagination had been too limited. In any case, that anyone could live in this grand place and call it "home" seemed beyond her comprehension. And now *she* would be living here.

A wave of homesickness, a longing for the cozy comfort of the Karska's humble dwelling with its bare simplicity on their familiar, narrow street, choked off her breath. Oh God, what had she done?

Interrupting her anxiety, the Genesis story about Rebekah popped into her mind. Had Rebekah felt this way? The account in the Bible didn't say. But she knew Rebekah had made a decision and stuck by it, facing her new life straight on. She'd gone with Eleazar without hesitation, and she'd become Isaac's wife.

With Rebekah as her example, Veronika decided she could face the changes in her own life with the same courage, for it was God who would provide her with strength. A sense of kinship with Rebekah pushed out her fears. She would trust God. Just like Rebekah. Taking a deep breath, she hurried to keep step with David.

As they passed through open double doors into the great room, Veronika's fear again threatened to overwhelm her. The vast room featured a monstrous stone fireplace that mouthed a veritable forest fire! And each of the magnificent tapestries covering the walls could hide the entire front of the Karska's house. And then there was Dagmar, wildly gesticulating as she told Lord and Lady Branden—Veronika recognized them both—that their son and his wife had just arrived. The shock and dismay on David's parents' faces was obvious. And daunting.

"What is it? What's wrong?" David cried, squeezing her hand reassuringly even as he expressed his alarm and disappointment. "Why aren't you happy to see us?"

Dagmar disappeared out the door as David's father's fingers convulsively gripped the lion paws on the ends of his chair arms before he slowly rose and came toward them. His wooden heels thudding on the stone tiles unexpectedly reminded Veronika of a funeral procession clacking over the cobblestones in New Town's city square. A tremor shook her body.

When Lord Branden stopped a short distance from them, Veronika stared at him in shock. His eyes were red-rimmed and bloodshot—from tears or lack of sleep; she had no way of knowing. His deep voice shook like a leaf vibrating in the wind. "Lucina—" his voice broke. He cleared his throat and tried again. "Lucina is—very ill. She may not—live."

Pain distorted his face and he bit his lips together in an effort to maintain his dignity. "The doctor thinks it could be another outbreak of the Black Death." He passed his hand over his face in the familial gesture of distress.

"We—we wrote to tell you—not to come. We didn't want either of you to risk taking sick." His beseeching eyes begged them to understand. Lady Branden moved to stand beside him, and he clutched her hand, pressing it to his heart as if it were his only link to hope.

Veronika's heart sank to her toes. The last thing she wanted to do was add to this family's distress. When David's arm slipped around her shoulders, she fixed her eyes on his face. She felt like an intruder, witnessing their grief.

"We never got your letter." David started strong but his voice sank to a shaky whisper. "Are you sure there's no hope?"

When his parents' expressions remained grim and neither of them readily responded, David hurried on, "Well, we *are* here, so we'll have to make the best of the situation and pray to God to keep us in good health."

He drew Veronika closer. "I want you to meet Veronika, my wife. As I wrote you, we were married almost three weeks ago." He bent his head and pressed an affectionate kiss on her cheek.

When Veronika's gaze met Lady Branden's, her new mother-in-law exclaimed, "Why, you're the pretty maid who chose the yellow rose bush for me." Gladness replaced the anguish on her face. "I didn't realize you were David's Veronika because I didn't know your name—but I should have guessed."

Veronika's eyes popped open wide and her heart jolted in her chest. David had referred to the significance of yellow roses early in their acquaintance, but it had been so long ago that she'd forgotten. She resolved to ask him about it when they were alone.

Stretching out her arms, Lady Branden embraced Veronika warmly. "Welcome, my dear. Forgive us for our shock; I'm afraid we've been terribly rude. This is an anxious time right now, with Lucina so ill, and we only meant to keep you safe."

When Lady Branden released Veronika and

turned to hug her son, Lord Branden greeted her with a smile and a hearty kiss on each cheek. "Welcome to the family. We were so happy for David when he wrote us about you."

Lady Branden gave a quick tug on the bell cord. "You must be hungry. I'll have something brought in for you to eat." She turned toward the housekeeper waiting discreetly in the background. "And Dagmar, see that the green guest room is ready for them."

Lord Branden enlisted David's help to relocate a small settee, placing it between the two heavily carved chairs he and his wife had been sitting in when David and Veronika arrived. He motioned for the young couple to be seated on the settee, and the four of them settled close together facing the fire.

Turning to his mother, his low voice filled with tenderness, David asked, "So, tell me, truly, how is Lucina?"

"Oh, David," Lady Branden sighed, unable to mask her sadness and fear, "she coughs and coughs. What she brings up is thick and stringy—like yarn. Her cheeks are covered with fine red lines, and more appear after each coughing spell. And she hardly sleeps. We've propped her up with pillows to help her breathe, but when she relaxes, she chokes and starts coughing again. She's so weak she can no longer get up without help. And then yesterday, two of the maids began coughing. We're afraid . . ." Lady Branden pressed her fingers to her trembling lips as her voice broke.

David, seated on Veronika's left, reached for her hand. As she extended her fingers to meet his, the firelight caught her mother's unusual little ring.

Lord Branden gasped. In the next instant, his tight, grating words hissed through his clenched teeth. "Where did you get that ring?"

Veronika lifted bewildered eyes to her new father-in-law's burning blue ones. "I-It was m-my mother's, my lord," she stammered, nervously trying to tug her hand away from David's clasp.

"And where did she get it?" Lord Branden's voice sharpened and distress gouged deep lines in his forehead and face.

Startled at being addressed in such an overtly aggressive manner, Veronika's soft voice quavered as she struggled to answer respectfully, "I-I don't know, my lord. My mother died shortly after I was born."

"And your father," he demanded harshly. "Tell me about your father."

243

By now, Veronika was shaking from head to toe. But she lifted her chin and answered bravely, "He was killed by a runaway carriage. I was told he had a wooden leg and couldn't move fast enough to get out of the way."

Like a coiled spring, Lord Branden sprang from his chair, ignoring it as it tipped over and clattered heavily against the marble floor. Veronika gasped as he grabbed David by his shoulders and jerked him to his feet. "What have you done?" he shouted, ruthlessly shaking his son. "Brought the enemy into our household?"

For all of his shock, David remained surprisingly calm. He raised his arms and pushed determinedly against his father's chest. Using a formal address, he responded mildly, "Father—what are you talking about?"

As if he'd been struck, Lord Branden fell back several steps, the flaming rage dying out of his eyes. He wiped a trembling hand over his face.

Lady Branden, suddenly appearing old and frail, slumped in her chair, while Dagmar swiftly and unobtrusively darted in and righted Lord Branden's fallen chair.

Stunned by her new father-in-law's bizarre outburst, Veronika sat frozen on the settee.

David took a bold step toward his father.

Recalling David's confrontation with Boris when he had insulted her, Veronika felt a sudden wave of fear that her husband would strike his father. She started to shake again. What kind of family had she married into?

But although David's words were low and intense, she had nothing to fear; he was firm but respectful.

"Veronika is my wife, Father. If you have a question about her family or her character, you will address it to me—in a civilized manner." Never in his life had David spoken up to his father, but he had become a man in the years away—and his very future at Burg Mosel stood in jeopardy.

Lady Branden's lips moved in a frantic, silent prayer, and her slender hands gripped the arms of her chair as if they were her only hold on reality.

Lord Branden sank into his chair, pale and shaken, but his sanity had returned. Sucking in a shuddering breath, he collected his dignity with visible effort and turned to Veronika. His eyes, so like David's, were grave and contrite.

"Forgive me, Veronika. Something inside of me snapped when I saw your ring." He swallowed hard and steadied his gravelly voice. "Jacques Monet, the man who tried to kill Kitty, wore a ring exactly like it." His shoulders heaved. "And when you said your father had a wooden leg—Jacques lost a leg due to frostbite."

His hands curled tensely around the lion's paws at the end of his chair arms, but he went on, "He was also responsible for my father's death. And his father, Pierre, killed my grandmother."

With a low moan, he continued, "I'm afraid all the anguish and sorrow he caused our family exploded in me when I saw your ring. I left Jacques in Nuremberg to be brought to justice, and I thought I'd dealt with all these feelings years ago." He wiped his hand over his face and squeezed his temples between his thumb and fingertips.

After a moment, Lord Branden looked up, his blue eyes almost gray with bleakness. "There is no excuse for my rash and insulting behavior, and I most sincerely beg your forgiveness." His eyes pleaded with her for mercy.

He looked so like David and acted so like David when in distress—brushing his hand over his face and squeezing his temples—that Veronika felt her shock give way to tenderness.

"Of course I forgive you, my lord. I never knew my father, so I cannot tell you whether or not his name was Jacques Monet, but on behalf of *my* good name, would you not hold his wrongs against me?"

Lord Branden whispered thickly, "How could I do otherwise when you have forgiven me for such unpardonable behavior?"

He turned to his son, "David, my anger was unjust and inexcusable. Can you forgive me?"

"Oh, Papa," David choked on the childhood name. Dropping to his knees beside his father, he threw his arms around the older man's neck. "We'll consider that it never happened."

Lord Branden leaned his forehead against his son's shoulder as he returned the embrace.

When servants entered the room, bearing trays laden with food, Lady Branden slowly released her grip on the arms of her chair and rose to direct them.

After a lengthy hug, David and his father stood to their feet. David reached down to Veronika and pulled her up and in close to his side. Lord Branden reached out his hand and rested it gently on her shoulder, his tender touch doing more to reassure her than his apology. She turned her head and lifted her chin, meeting his contrite gaze with a smile.

* * *

In the bed in the guest chamber, Veronika lay wrapped in David's arms.

"Are you all right, my love?" he whispered against her cheek. "You don't hate me for the way my father behaved?"

Anxious to reassure her young husband, Veronika stroked his cheek and replied softly, "No, David. I'm sure it was just a mistake. Besides, your parents have been under an incredible strain with your sister so sick. And your father apologized most humbly. Really, you look very like him. I couldn't help but love him for that, if for no other reason."

Satisfied with her reassurance, David kissed her cheek and relaxed into sleep.

Veronika, however, lay awake late into the night, the afternoon's events replaying over and over in her mind. For the first time in her life, she felt sincere curiosity about her parentage. Who *was* her father?

What kind of man was he? Why did he have a wooden leg? And what about her mother's little ring—could it have belonged to the wicked man who'd caused her husband's family such outrageous grief?

Dear God, it was daunting enough to have married into this noble family. Truly, she'd had no idea, indeed, never could have imagined the grandeur, the wealth, the power that formed David's heritage.

Seeing him against his natural backdrop explained a lot about him that she'd naively attributed to a naturally charming personality. She understood much more clearly now why he'd stood out from the other university men who over the years had come and gone from At The Stone Swan.

The more she thought about her situation, the more overwhelmed she felt. Her heart began to pound and fear threatened to suffocate her—fear that she'd prove inadequate for the position in which she'd unwittingly placed herself. She lifted her head; she needed space, she needed air. But moving would wake David. And then she'd have to explain to him her restlessness.

Then strongly into her fear came the words from Genesis:

> *"And they blessed Rebekah and said unto her,*
> *'Thou art our sister, be the mother of thousands*
> *of millions, and let thy seed possess*
> *the gate of those which hate them.'"*

It was a moment of epiphany; just as God had used Rebekah to bring a blessing to her new family, she would ask God to show her how to be a blessing to David's family. Taking comfort in her new-found purpose, she breathed a prayer, "Dear Father, help me show your love to David's family."

With God's help she could face the truth of her heritage. And with God's help she would accept the challenge that being part of David's family presented to her. Even as Rebekah had done for her Isaac.

As she relaxed and closed her eyes, confident that God had heard her request, her husband's gentle breathing lulled her to sleep.

* * *

In the master suite, Lady Branden prepared for bed. She felt at a loss to know how to broach the evening's events. Her husband's startling outburst was only one of her worries. She also needed to decide if David and Veronika should be permitted to visit Lucina. Normally, she would have consulted her husband, but she had to admit feeling apprehensive about bringing up anything that might cause him further distress, for fear it might force him to talk about the information Veronika had given them before he felt ready. She knew it would be easy for both of them to express opinions they would later regret or to reach conclusions that may alter when seen in a different light.

* * *

When his wife slipped into bed beside him, Lord Branden pretended to be asleep. Although he'd smoothed the situation over on the surface, the inner struggle triggered by Veronika's ring continued to torment him. He would know that ring anywhere. It was a most unique piece of jewelry. And he'd gotten a clear look at it. No, there could be no doubt. Not when combined with the other facts Veronika had given regarding her father's wooden leg and her family name. She was undoubtedly Jacques Monet's daughter. Thankfully, she didn't look like him. But still, how was he to deal with the emotions such knowledge evoked? Oh, he'd reconciled to his father's death and made his peace with God on that count, but there'd been the grief, the long years of his mother's widowhood, and the responsibilities thrust upon him without preparation or transition.

Thinking about the past brought up all the old feelings of self-blame. If only he hadn't so impulsively invited Jacques to be their guest at Burg Mosel, his father might not have met such an untimely death. If only . . . If only . . .

And he couldn't escape the present situation. There was no way to send the girl away to allow him time and space to work through his feelings; she was David's wife. She would be living with them. He would see her every day. She was family!

He would go crazy if he thought any more about it. Yet he couldn't *not* think about it. He had to face it. Deal with it. Find a way to live at peace with it.

Should he talk to Kitty? How she must despise him. Never in all his life had he so shamed her. Could she even find it in her heart to respect him again? No, he couldn't talk to anyone about his feelings, especially not to his wife, not until he'd come to some resolve. If she rejected him, he couldn't bear that as well as the inner turmoil. Better to let time pass and hope it would soften her memory of his disgusting exhibition.

Captive to his despairing thoughts, Lord Branden rolled onto his side. But sleep was long in coming.

Joyce Brandt Williams

CHAPTER SIXTEEN

Veronika hoped she didn't show the dismay she felt at seeing the changes in the beautiful girl who had visited Prague with her family more than two years ago. Lucina had been healthy then—rosy color in her cheeks, spunk in her green eyes, girlish roundness to her figure.

Now her cheeks were gaunt and streaked with tiny red lines from broken blood vessels. Dark circles surrounded her sunken eyes and her hair had lost its luster. And her body, elevated by pillows so she could breathe without expending the effort required to hold herself upright, was little more than skin stretched over bones.

David stepped close to his sister and lightly brushed her shoulder with his fingertips. "Lucina, dear, it's David."

The girl's shadowed eyelids slowly opened.

Watching her drawn face light with pleasure brought tears to Veronika's eyes.

"Oh, David, I've missed you," Lucina whispered, her hands fluttering on the duvet covering her lap.

David dropped to his knees and caught her pale, thin hands in his own large ones. "You always wanted a sister," he turned his head and beckoned to Veronika, "so I brought you one. This is Veronika. She's my wife."

As Veronika knelt beside Lucina, she looked up. "I'm so glad—" Violent coughing broke off her words.

Agatha, Lucina's maid, who had been sitting quietly to one side, quickly jumped up and rushed to the girl. "You must leave at once!"

Her reproachful order sent them scurrying for the door.

In the corridor, David turned stricken eyes on his wife. "What—what can we do?"

Inadequacy overwhelmed Veronika; how could she possibly comfort her husband? If only she had thought to bring some of Eva's herbs!

Impulsively, she wrapped her arms tightly around him. "We can pray," she whispered, infusing her words with far more confidence than she felt.

"Yes, we can pray," he echoed, but his voice sounded hollow, and Veronika knew God's mercy was their only hope.

As they made their way to the chapel, Veronika reached for David's hand, hoping her touch would give him courage. Inside the sanctuary, they walked side-by-side down the aisle and sat close together in the front. David immediately closed his eyes and moved his lips in silent prayer.

After praying earnestly for Lucina's recovery, Veronika raised her head and looked around. Her gaze took in the frescoes, the candles, the stained glass window depicting a blue-robed Shepherd cradling a small white lamb in His arms. But it was the Book of Hours on the marble-topped altar that inexplicably drew her. Recalling David telling her his grandmother used to read to him and his sister from the book when he was a boy, she rose from her place beside David, moved out into the aisle, and slipped around the altar railing.

Light from the window caught in the facets of the ruby adorning the book's cover; it sparkled with an unspoken invitation. Veronika's pulse quickened. Her fingers trembled as she unfastened the heavy, ornate clasp. Cautiously, she raised the ivory cover. When the leather binding creaked slightly, she darted a glance at David, but his head was still bowed and he didn't stir.

Returning her attention to the book, Veronika turned the first two pages. When she discovered the faded yellow rose pressed against the presentation page, she impulsively pinched the brittle stem between her thumb and index finger and lifted the parchment-thin flower.

In that moment, a sudden thought jarred her memory. Could this yellow rose have some bearing on David's enigmatical remarks so long ago and his mother's reference last night to the yellow rose bush?

* * *

Lord Branden left early and stayed out late, riding over the land, visiting with the villagers, speaking with the croppers. He inspected the stables and talked with the servants. He felt a desperate urgency to keep busy; surely activity would divert his thoughts from the agony in his soul.

But the presence of Jacques Monet's daughter, however virtuous she might prove to be, still clawed at the edges of his waking thoughts and viciously tormented his sleep. Several nights in a row, he'd awakened with a start to find himself drenched in sweat but unable to remember what he'd dreamed.

Tonight, his dream had replayed his trip with his father to Nuremberg to deliver Jacques Monet to Magistrate Wolf for justice. He relived sitting beside his father in the sleigh. He saw his father's wind-reddened cheeks and frosted eyebrows. He experienced again his panic when his father clutched his chest. And terror engulfed him when his mind replayed his father's collapse.

Trapped in his nightmare, he jerked upright, wheezing as he sucked in desperate, gasping breaths. His flailing arms struck the bedclothes, jarring him awake. He shook from head to toe, his body dripping with perspiration.

Dim moonlight filtered through the tall, narrow bedroom window and illuminated his sleeping wife. He heaved a rattling sigh and sank back down on the bed. If he wasn't careful, he'd wake her. And she'd ask questions. Questions he didn't want to answer. Questions he didn't know *how* to answer.

Tossing about in his mind to explain the anguish he'd thought he'd dealt with years ago, Lord Branden finally concluded that believing Jacques Monet had been brought to justice had enabled him to put the whole subject out of his mind without ever facing the betrayal he'd suffered. It had obviously been a false security; Jacques had either been released or he'd escaped. Knowing Jacques, he suspected the latter.

He rolled onto his side, his thoughts coming full circle. He had no escape. Veronika was his son's wife, and he would have to accept her. He'd gone over all this a million times already. But a person's sin didn't only affect the sinner, it hurt everyone around him. In their case, Jacques's sin would now affect them *forever* because their son had married Jacques's daughter. Dear God, would this bitter saga never end?

The bed seemed full of lumps. Lord Branden shifted, trying to find a comfortable position.

His wife stirred. "Mmmm," she let out her breath. He froze.

"Are you all right, my love?" she murmured sleepily.

"I had a bad dream and can't seem to go back to sleep." That was the truth, a mild version of it.

"Could I get you a drink?" she offered, obviously awake now. "Or would it help to talk?" Often, when he faced a difficult decision, he found peace and clarity in his wife's willingness to listen.

"No. No drink."

He lay silent for a moment, contemplating. What did he have to lose? He'd already lost his peace of mind. Surely, Kitty loved him enough to bear with him through his struggle.

He rose up on one elbow. "I-I'm having a hard time," he confessed.

"Yes?" She lay very still, waiting for him to continue.

"Kitty, our son married Jacques Monet's daughter! Jacques Monet! The man who tried to kill you! I was so confident Magistrate Wolf would see justice done that I put the whole episode out of my mind. But that obviously didn't happen." A groan erupted from the depths of his soul.

"And now," he pounded the duvet with his fist, "our David has married Jacques's daughter." He shuddered and dropped back down on the bed with a despairing thud. "So there's no end. Ever."

Although age and responsibility had tempered Kitty's spirited nature, sometimes her outspokenness still came to the fore. She sat up abruptly, turned toward him in the pale light, and spoke forcefully, "Yes, there is an end, Nick. You can *forgive* Jacques."

"Forgive Jacques!" Propelled by the force of his exclamation, he reared up beside her and barked, "What good would that do? It won't bring my father back—or undo our son's marriage." He thumped back on the bed, defending himself in a flat tone, "Besides, Jacques is dead."

Kitty took a deep breath and then spoke the hard words as gently as she could, "Not to you, he isn't."

Her words stabbed his heart. She'd spoken the truth. Nick wiped his hand over his face, as if to erase the bitterness she'd exposed. His shoulders heaved under the weight of his burden, and his chest screamed with pent-up emotion.

"Let me tell you something that happened this morning. Maybe it will change how you feel about Veronika."

Kitty let her breath out softly as she began. "I went to the chapel, intending to pray. When I got to the door, I suddenly thought that I should have asked David and Veronika to join me. I'd already pushed the door open a crack, just enough so I could see into the chapel, and I was surprised to find they were already there. David was sitting in the front with his head bowed and Veronika was standing behind the altar.

She had opened the Book of Hours—and what do you think she was holding? The yellow rose pressed by your great-grandmother! I was so shocked, I just stared. While I watched, Veronika looked at David. I thought she was going to say something to him, but she didn't; she just studied the rose, turning it over and over.

"Then David looked up—and Veronika said, 'Do you remember the first time you came to our Fellowship meeting at the Jamikovi's? You told me it was significant that I'd given your mother a yellow rose bush. And you asked me if I'd like to know why.' When David nodded, Veronika said, 'At the time, I thought you were trying to flirt with me, so I told you I had no interest in you or your yellow roses.'"

Lady Branden interrupted her tale to comment to her husband, "Oh, I knew I was eavesdropping, but I kept listening anyway."

Lord Branden lay perfectly still with his eyes closed, wishing his wife would think he'd fallen asleep. But she didn't take the hint.

"Well, then David told her that on the night your mother, Lady Rosamund, met Erik, your father, she found a yellow rose pressed in The Book of Hours.

And years later, God used the same pressed rose to assure your mother that she didn't need to worry about your future—or my interest in Jacques."

Nick twitched the edge of the comforter impatiently. Why was his wife dredging up things he'd rather forget?

Kitty, obviously sensing his restiveness, plunged quickly ahead, "Do you remember, when we were in Prague, the maid from At The Stone Swan chose a yellow rose bush for me . . . the one I planted by the stone bench in the garden?"

He grunted, not caring if his irritation showed.

"Well, that maid," she paused for emphasis, "was Veronika."

Startled, Nick opened his eyes; she had his full attention.

"Did you know that David was watching out the second story window when Veronika gave me that rose bush?"

Nick tried to stifle his annoyed groan.

"And that's not all. When I asked David about it later, he told me that at one point he was discouraged in his relationship with Veronika, but he ran into her unexpectedly, and she was holding a yellow rose. And that renewed his hope."

Nick rolled his eyes and moaned, "Oh, Kitty, it's all so subjective. Just feelings. Impressions. Thoughts." He threw out his arms. "How do I know everything I've always believed isn't just superstition? If only God would do a miracle."

Then, thinking better of his presumption, Nick quickly corrected himself, "Forget I said that. I know it's not right." His voice grew a shade livelier. "God can bring good out of bad. I *know* He can."

He sat up abruptly and turned to her, "Do you remember that awful day when you informed my mother that you weren't her slave?"

"Wha-a-at?" Kitty blinked hard at this sudden twist in the conversation.

"Well, do you remember?" he insisted, rising up on one elbow and leaning toward her. "You couldn't have been more than about nine or ten."

"Yes, I remember." Kitty's head drooped as she tasted her sadness all over again. "My mother had just died."

"Well, I remember it too. For another reason." Nick's voice was fully alive now and filled with a resurgence of energy and conviction. "I felt very angry for my parents' sake; they were so kind to you, and I resented your ingratitude. In fact, I was so angry that I told my father I wished he would send you away."

At her open-mouthed gasp of astonishment, Nick snorted sheepishly and reaffirmed, "Yes, I did." He sobered, "And do you know what he said to me? He said I shouldn't resent you. That if I wasn't careful, I'd find myself resenting all the hard things in life that I didn't understand." He hesitated, then sighed moodily, "He was right, wasn't he?"

Speechless at his confession, Kitty only managed a weak agreement.

"And look how that situation turned out!" His chuckle was rich with meaning. "You've been the biggest blessing in my entire life. But I couldn't have guessed it at the time." He fell silent for a moment before concluding, "Maybe this situation with Veronika will prove to be a blessing too."

He heaved a weighty sigh and reached for his wife, pulling her into his arms as he confessed, "Thank you for being honest with me. You're right, I do need to forgive Jacques—and I will, as God is my witness."

CHAPTER SEVENTEEN

Veronika looked into the large, nearly empty trunk she'd been determined to unpack. A full week had passed since she and David arrived at Burg Mosel. They'd continued sleeping in the green guest chamber until yesterday, when the suite being prepared for them in the north wing was pronounced ready. Their belongings had been transferred to their permanent accommodations, and now she could finally see the bottom of the last trunk.

David had gone riding this morning while she'd stayed behind to finish unpacking her things. She felt glad to be alone—with her belongings as well as her thoughts. Her few simple dresses now hung on the pegs in the dressing room. Beneath them, the toes of her spare pair of shoes pointed to the wall. Her undergarments were neatly folded and stored on a shelf. The elegant comb and brush set, among the gifts David had presented to her as wedding presents, was now arranged with pride and care on the dressing table. The new Bible sat on the bedside table, waiting to be taken to the chapel. Three pieces of hand-worked linen, received as wedding gifts and carefully packed to preserve their beauty, were now displayed, one under the dresser set on the dressing table, one on the bedside table, and one over the back of a chair. A folded length of fabric for a new dress rested on the floor beside her.

Only two parcels remained in the chest, and Veronika didn't immediately recognize either of them. The larger parcel was wrapped in fabric—the skirt-front of a once-favorite indigo blue *cotte* that had become too worn to be respectable. But Jana never wasted anything, and Jana had helped with the packing.

Come to think of it, Jana had mentioned placing a couple of parcels in the trunk—one from her and one from Eva. In the excitement of the trip and meeting her new family, with the consternation her ring had caused, in addition to Lucina's illness, she'd quite forgotten Jana's comment until now.

Tears blurred Veronika's vision as she lifted out the package from Jana. The soft wool fabric bunched and slipped off, revealing the battered metal box that had belonged to her mother. Veronika suddenly sat very still. Tied around the box, a length of black thread secured a folded piece of parchment to the top. She held it in her hands and stared at it for a long time. Could the words on this paper—or the contents of this box—spell an end to her happiness here?

Oh, things had been smoothed over that first evening, but she sensed a residual undercurrent of tension. Lord Branden seemed to avoid her. He wasn't rude; he just didn't stay in her company for very long at a time. She knew if she said anything to David, he would think her fears were unfounded. But she couldn't help how she felt.

She sank down on the rug with the box in her lap and tugged at the thread until it broke. She would know the truth.

The stiff piece of parchment crackled as she unfolded it. Two names leaped up at her: Margot Karlova and Jacques Monet. It was a marriage contract.

She smashed the paper into her lap in one swift, involuntary movement. Shaking, cold, with a suffocating sickness in her soul, she lost sight of David's love, of God's love. Now she knew the truth: David's family had just cause to hate her.

How long she sat there, paralyzed by shame and fear, she didn't know. But when sharp footsteps approaching in the corridor interrupted her torment, they startled her back to reality. With a quick swipe, she hastily smothered the marriage certificate and the metal box in the old skirt fabric, rose to her knees, and stuffed them back into the trunk.

On an impulse, she pulled out the other parcel—the one she guessed was from Eva—and deposited it on the floor beside her. She managed to lower the trunk lid just as the footsteps reached the door.

Sinking back on her heels, Veronika grabbed up the large parcel and slipped off its brown cambric wrapping.

As David entered the room, she looked up. "Did you have a nice ride?" She hoped her voice didn't betray her recent panic.

"I did," he said, moving toward her with the chill of outdoors and the smell of horse lather still clinging to his clothes.

Dropping her eyes to the parcel in her hands, she saw that it was a large, straw-colored muslin drawstring bag. Endeavoring to buy time to regain her inner composure, she smiled and held it out to David. "Could you please open this for me?"

David grinned, sniffed the bag appreciatively, and then easily opened it. "Seeing to it I'm useful, are you?" he chuckled as he bent over to kiss her.

Although she raised her face to meet his kiss, her blush came more from relief than from his teasing.

"I stopped in to see Lucina before I went riding." He shook his head and heaved a discouraged sigh as he handed the opened bag back to Veronika. "It seems to me she's getting worse. I wish there was something I could do for her."

While David was still speaking, Veronika stood to her feet and carried the muslin bag to the bed. Up-ending it, she shook out its contents with a couple of sharp, jerking motions.

"What are these?" she exclaimed softly, surprised by the assortment of smaller drawstring bags that plopped onto the blue duvet. Strong herbal scents filled the air and tickled her nose, and she sneezed. Then picking up the bags, one after another, she pressed each one, sniffing, trying to determine their contents. Each bag was numbered and there were numerous bags bearing each number from one through six.

Jumbled in the heap, she found a note from Eva in her spidery script. With a soft cry of delight, Veronika read the precious words:

My dear girl, You have been the daughter I never had, and although I am rejoicing in your marriage to David, I shall miss you terribly. In your new life, you will face many challenges. I know you are strong and brave, but sometimes that is not enough. I hope that this collection of my herbs will be a blessing. On the back of this note are the numbers one through six, and beside each number is an ailment. The bags are labeled with corresponding numbers and contain my remedies.

Without finishing the rest of Eva's note, Veronika flipped it over and rapidly scanned the list: ague, rheumatism, fever, palsy, *congestion.*

"I've been praying every day that Lucina will get well . . ." At his wife's gasp, David interrupted himself to demand, "What is it?"

Too excited to speak, Veronika thrust the paper toward her bewildered husband.

David raised his brows as he took the paper, but before he could question her further, Veronika pointed eagerly to number five. "Look—for congestion!" She began grabbing up and then just as quickly, tossing aside the small muslin bags.

"Here. Here's a five." She waved the bag at him. And just as quickly as her heart had surged with hope, her face fell. "Wh-What do we do with it?" she whispered, pressing the bag to her heart.

David turned his attention from his distraught wife to the bag still clutched in her hand. Easing it from her grip, he turned it over. "Look! It says: 'Add water to form a paste. Apply to chest. Repeat every three hours.'" He grabbed her hand and dashed toward the door.

"Whoa . . . where are you going?" Veronika squealed, scrambling to keep up with him.

"To find my mother . . ."

* * *

When Veronika opened the door to Lucina's room in response to David's knock, a strong, herbaceous odor struck him in the face. He wrinkled up his nose, but his eyes filled with a hopeful light.

"Well?" he whispered, obviously anxious to know if the first herbal treatment had been effective.

Hearing David's voice, Lady Branden came up behind Veronika. The two women stepped into the corridor and Veronika closed the door behind them.

273

"Lucina's resting," Lady Branden said quietly. She hesitated before conceding, "We think she's a little better. Her breathing seems less labored. But it's hard to tell." She shook her head. "We don't want to get our hopes up too soon."

"I-I've been praying for a miracle. God does do miracles—sometimes—I've heard . . ."

At the word miracle, Lady Branden's countenance took on a wary look; that was the precise word Nick had used last night when he wanted God to prove Himself. But now, all she said was: "Keep praying. Perhaps God will choose to be merciful to us."

The next evening, after a day and a half of herbal treatments, Lady Branden and Veronika joined Lord Branden and David for the evening meal. The women were both tired and reeked of horehound, oregano, and thyme, but they cautiously agreed that Lucina had definitely improved; she was expelling more mucous each time she coughed, and she had slept for several continuous hours.

* * *

It was nearly bedtime. Lord Branden sat in his large carved chair in the great room, staring into the fire. Lady Branden was upstairs helping Agatha prepare Lucina for the night. David and Veronika sat close together on the settee.

It was the first time since her arrival that Veronika had felt relaxed enough to study the elegant furnishings and accessories—richly embroidered green velvet draperies, delicate chairs, brocade-covered settees, marble-topped tables displaying *objets d'art*. The jade bust of a young woman on a round pedestal table in the center of the room piqued her interest. After a few moments, her gaze moved to the canvas that filled the space above the fireplace. It depicted a young woman who markedly resembled her husband.

The exception to the room's grandeur and rich furnishings was a simple, low, wooden stool that sat askew near the fireplace—as if it had been impatiently scooted out of the way.

Veronika suddenly thought she would feel more comfortable squatting on that little stool near the fire than perched on the elegant settee. It was going to take some effort to grow accustomed to living in such splendor. As her thoughts wandered into the past, a wave of nostalgia swept over her, a longing for days of simplicity and security.

She shifted her gaze to her new husband and requested wistfully, "David, would you play some of the hymns we sang at Fellowship? I'm missing the singing."

"All right, but you'll have to sing with me." He stood and pulled her up beside him.

While David pushed back the heavy draperies covering the entrance to the music salon, Veronika took a burning candle from the great room and lit the tapers in the stand behind the harpsichord bench. David lowered his lean body into his familiar place on the bench and ran his fingers lightly over the keys.

While he played softly and sang the words of several psalms set to music and then progressed to a couple of hymns written over the years by Jan Hus's followers, Veronika let her eyes wander around the small chamber joining the great room. Rose-grained marble panels covered the walls. A small table topped with a forest green bowl filled with dried lavender buds and flanked by two padded ladies' chairs formed a conversation area to one side. The harpsichord sat at the center of a sunburst of colorful mosaic tiles that covered the floor. The reflection of the candle flames as they danced on the instrument's gleaming surface prompted her to reach out and smooth her hand over the polished wood.

David's rich tenor inspired Veronika to join him with her sweet soprano. Their words and harmony blended, filling Veronika's heart with a sense of peace as they sang together, *"Fairest Lord Jesus, ruler of all nature . . ."*

* * *

Their young voices carried into the great room and their music touched a tender place in Lord Branden's heart. He'd been an accomplished musician in his youth, but over the years he'd played less and less. While they sang, he mused on the fact that he'd played less frequently as his faith had grown cold. Could there be a connection between faith and worship? He closed his eyes and leaned his head against the lion's head in the crest of his chair. God seemed very close.

From the deepest place in his heart, he breathed a prayer, "Forgive me, God, for harboring bitterness. Give me Your love for Veronika." Heaving a weighty sigh, he released his burden of resentment and sorrow, and reached up to rub away the moisture that had somehow collected in the corners of his eyes.

* * *

Morning brought with it sunshine, the first since David and Veronika had arrived at Burg Mosel. After a breakfast of millet porridge and raisins, David invited, "Come, my love. I want to show you something."

Veronika had spent most of the past two days assisting Lady Branden in administering the herbal treatments, and David had sat in the chapel for hours, praying. But last night, when the two women had left Lucina sleeping peacefully under the watchful care of Agatha, Lady Branden suggested Veronika spend the morning with David; he wanted to give her a tour of his home. She promised to find them and report any changes or improvements after she checked on her daughter.

David took Veronika's hand and urged her past the chapel to the stone steps leading to the tower.

She followed him up the stairs and stopped beside him when he halted half-way to the top. With a whispered, "Watch," he knelt and pressed on a stone in the corner of the step directly above the one they stood on. As David straightened up, the wall grated, moving to expose a cold, dark, dry-smelling cavern.

Although Veronika recoiled, she remained silent in her trepidation. But she clutched David's arm so lightly her fingers bruised his flesh.

As he recounted his great-grandmother's fate, horror suffused her face. And when he described how his mother, too, had been locked in the secret chamber and left to die, her father-in-law's outburst their first evening at Burg Mosel acquired new significance.

"David," she cried, turning away from him as her secret agony burst from her lips, "that man, Jacques Monet—h-he was my father."

David raised his brows and soothed indulgently. "You don't know that, my love."

Veronika's voice rose with her despair. "Yes! Yes, I do. Just before I found the bag of herbs from Eva, I found my parents' marriage certificate in a package that Jana put in my trunk." She swung back to face him, her face reflecting her anguish. "Oh, David, how could your parents ever overlook that enough to love me?" She broke into convulsive sobbing.

Too stunned to answer, David pulled her rigid, resistant figure into his arms and awkwardly rubbed her stiffened back.

"I couldn't help overhearing you, Veronika." Lord Branden's words startled them; they hadn't heard him follow them down the hallway and stop at the bottom of the stairway in time to hear Veronika's confession. They raised their heads and stared down at him as he began climbing the steps.

He didn't speak again until he reached the wide step just below them. He met Veronika's gaze directly, and said, "I want you to know that you are right, Veronika. In my own strength, I could never get past the resentment, the bitterness, the desire for revenge."

His voice shook as he continued, "But God demonstrated something beyond revenge when he offered us forgiveness and redemption. By loving us and forgiving our sins against Him, He enables us— well, more personally, He has enabled *me* to forgive Jacques. And that has set me free to love you."

He patted Veronika's shoulder. "What happened in the past was not your fault, my dear." His eyes blazed with sincerity and he spoke confidently, "And I believe good will result from this situation. You'll see."

Tapping footsteps in the hallway below diverted their attention. The three of them swung around to see who was approaching them in such haste. When Lady Branden emerged from the corridor and saw them on the stairs, her face brightened with relief. Although she tried to speak, she only managed to gasp out unintelligible sounds as she rushed up the steps.

"What is it?" Lord Branden demanded tensely when his wife stopped beside him, panting to catch her breath.

Lady Branden's cheeks glowed and her green eyes sparkled. "I-It's Lucina. She's better. Truly, she's better. She slept all night," her words came out in an excited rush, "and she's breathing freely this morning. She even asked for breakfast. It's the first time in over two weeks that she's requested food. And she brushed her own hair. Come. See for yourselves."

When they reached Lucina's suite, Lady Branden tapped lightly on the door. As Agatha opened it, they all heard Lucina's weak voice call, "Come in."

David and Veronika surged forward, following Lady Branden into the room. But Lord Branden

281

startled everyone. He took one look at Lucina's smiling face then strode across the room. Falling to his knees beside his daughter, he began to weep— great, wracking sobs that wrenched his entire body.

Lady Branden wilted into a nearby chair. Agatha hovered anxiously by the bedside table. And David wrapped his arms around his wife, he said later "to keep her from fainting," but of course everyone knew it was to keep himself on his feet.

Lucina put out her thin hand and girlishly patted her father's bowed head while everyone watched. Waited. "I love you, Papa," she whispered.

Lord Branden's sobs gradually subsided. He lifted his head and looked around at them through tear-drenched eyes. His wife. His daughter. His son. And his son's wife—the daughter of their enemy.

"God *has* brought good out of our tragedy. He sent us Veronika to bring healing. And not just to Lucina," he quickly amended, "but to our whole family. To me." His face shone with an inner light. "We have, this very day, surely witnessed a miracle.

EPILOGUE

While Lord Branden paced and Lucina skipped up and down the corridor, David shifted uncomfortably on the straight-backed chair positioned against the wall in the hallway outside the suite of rooms he'd shared with Veronika for the past year. Restless, he scooted the chair several inches away from the wall and leaned it back, balancing it on two legs—just like a boy. Closing his eyes, he sucked in a ragged breath. But the tension did not leave his body. If anything, it intensified. The cries and moans of the past several hours had ceased. But the quiet that followed worried him even more.

And then the door flew open.

Agatha bustled out with a tightly wrapped bundle filling her arms. "You have a son," she proclaimed as David jumped to his feet, leaving his chair to clatter back down on all four legs.

Following behind Agatha, Lady Branden emerged carrying another bundle. "Twins!" she announced triumphantly as they placed one bundle in David's shaking arms and the other in his father's. "Two little boys to carry on the family name."

Lucina came running. "What shall we name them?" she burst out in excitement.

In the bedroom, Veronika leaned back on her pillow. Although she was tired, a peaceful smile rested on her face. God had given her a promise that first night at Burg Mosel, when fear had threatened to overcome her faith, and she repeated the words now, whispering them into the empty room.

"And they blessed Rebekah and said unto her,
'Thou art our sister, be the mother
of thousands of millions
and let thy seed possess the gate
of those which hate them.'"

Now the promise was a compounded one. Lucina was fully recovered. And she had presented David's family with not just one son, but two.

Just like Rebekah!

The End

Enjoy This Brief Excerpt from
Lady Alexandra,
Book Four In The Rose & The Ring Series:

Ivo Sloboda began moving toward the doorway where Lady Alexandra, the rightful owner of Hrad Bělá, stood eavesdropping in the dark. Terrified of being discovered, she turned and fled down the hallway. Darting into a seldom-used side room, she dropped to the floor and curled her too-thin form under a rough bench, hoping the corner shadows would provide her protection from her brother-in-law's anger. Tears welled up behind her eyes as she silently pleaded, *"Dear God, I've given everything I have in order to keep peace, except my very self. Must he demand that too?"*

ABOUT THE AUTHOR

Joyce Brandt Williams, whose family of three children has now grown to include five delightful grandchildren, lives in the beautiful Wenatchee Valley in Eastern Washington State. She and her pastor husband, Paul Williams, were married for forty-three years until his passing into the presence of God in January 2017. Joyce now devotes her life to her family, her church (where she serves as Pastor of Congregational Care), and her writing.

Joyce loves history and enjoys traveling, but writing is a long-held passion. Her first book, Lady Rosamund, was initially published by **Heartsong** as *The Lady Rose* and has, in the years since, grown into the moving series, **The Rose & The Ring**.

Follow Joyce on Amazon (http://www.amazon .com/author/joycebrandtwilliams), read her inspiring devotional blog at Joyce Williams Write Now, and connect with her on Facebook at Joyce Brandt Williams—Redemptive Rose Fiction.

See a list of other books by Joyce Brandt Williams on the following page.

OTHER BOOKS BY
JOYCE BRANDT WILLIAMS

Quilt of Grace,

a Western & Frontier tale of restoration and hope!

The Rose & The Ring

Made in the USA
Middletown, DE
08 September 2020

18566120R00172